THE
MYSTIC'S
WIFE

Cover artwork by Tima Lee

Book design by Sheer Design and Typesetting
Typeset in Bembo and Cinzel

First edition 2023

Paperback ISBN 978-0-6458360-2-8.

eBook ISBN 978-0-6458360-0-4

THE MYSTIC'S WIFE

LIVING WITH A FREE SPIRIT

A Novel *by* Tima Lee

EARTHENWARE BOOKS

CONTENTS

*The Tao that can be trodden
is not the enduring and unchanging Tao.*

THE START OF THE TAO TE CHING

PROLOGUE

Mei awoke with that urge, needing to go. "Oh no," she thought, getting up in a panic. She couldn't have another accident, not here. There was no warning any more, none at all. She brushed past the woman, tensing her whole body as she walked, straining to keep it in. She made it to the door and out to the simple facilities, just in time.

Stepping back into the warmth of the tiny cottage, she was about to start explaining her hasty exit but suddenly felt hot and flushed. She stopped and tried to control her breathing. A sudden convulsion gripped her and she was powerless to contain the explosion.

She stared down in horror at last night's half-digested meal now covering the floor. The taste of fishy bile in the back of her throat brought more retching. The wave passed and her breathing started to return to normal. Then, standing there faced by the expanse of lost food, the sobbing took hold as the weight of her desperate situation overwhelmed her.

The woman didn't seem overly concerned about the splatter of unpleasant slime that had just appeared in her home. She poured water onto a cloth and brought it to her guest for her to wipe her face and hands. She led Mei around the pool of sick, sat her down by the fire and brought her a cup of tea. She went outside to fetch a bowl of water and a rag, then set about clearing up the mess. When she had finished, she took the bowl outside and a while later came back in drying her hands.

"Did you try the tea?" she asked lightly. "I used to find it helped me in my pregnancies." She poured a cup for herself and joined her guest at the fireside.

Mei sipped the tea and took deep breaths. "I'm sorry, I thought the sickness had all finished."

The woman made light of the event, waving away the apology with a little shake of her head and a smile.

Mei felt truly grateful for the kindness of this stranger. She had been appreciating her hosts' kindness ever since her husband had knocked on their door the evening before, asking for directions to the old man's house. Already weary after walking from the town, Mei had been dismayed when they had said it was still a long way further up the valley. A great wave of relief had come over her when the couple had welcomed them into their home, insisting that they stay with them for the night before continuing their journey the following day.

There had been more relief that morning. Mei's husband had risen early and she heard him discussing the route with the man. It sounded daunting, but the man had suggested it might be better for her husband to meet with the old man alone, saying that Mei would be welcome to stay with them until he returned. Her husband had then left and Mei had been able to remain resting under the warm covers. Soon after, she heard the man leave to go fishing, the woman calling out after him, "And Chuey, no need to hurry home." Then, with one arm cradling her unborn child, Mei had drifted off into a deep sleep. And that is where she had stayed, until being abruptly woken by the pressing call of nature.

The woman sat in calm silence for a while, then asked gently, "How are you feeling now?"

The simple question brought more tears. Staring into space, Mei shook her head slowly back and forth. "I've made a terrible mistake."

The older woman didn't need to ask. She had already sensed her guest's regret at marrying the young philosopher. The tension between them had been apparent since the couple first arrived. From the conversation the night before, it was clear that the husband's single-minded pursuit of wisdom was not shared by his young wife. Mei's silent resentment at being dragged so far from home on her husband's quest had been plain.

Mei's face wrinkled up with the bitterness of her self-pity. Looking around the simple home, she said, "This isn't me! I, I, I just don't think I can ..." Another upswell of emotion saved her from having to say any more. Then, with a sigh and a sip her tea, Mei regained most of her composure. She looked at her host, and that is when she said it. "It's alright for you. You're so ... Well, you're so *right* for all this. I'm not!"

The older woman's eyebrows raised, as though she found this unexpected accusation amusing. It was very early in the day for wine, but she decided that this was one of those days when they wouldn't wait for the men to return. She fetched the jug and picked up a cup. As she reached for another, she looked back at Mei. She decided to leave the second cup where it was, feeling that her young guest would do better staying with the tea. She put a log on the fire and settled herself down, smiling at her own thoughts as she tried to decide where to begin. She took a sip of the wine and swallowed.

"So you think that I'm 'so right' for all of this, do you?" She gave a little laugh. "Well perhaps I should tell you *my* story."

1. FIRST IMPRESSIONS

People know me as Chuey's wife, but no one is just someone's wife. I haven't always been Chuey's wife and if my cousin hadn't introduced us at a funeral I'd probably never have become his wife. I didn't even want to go.

The funeral was in a neighbouring village. When we arrived, we found that it was being held outside, on a patch of ground between two small houses, next to what seemed like an animal pen. It was a small gathering and the mourners were dressed casually, some looking as though they had just wandered in from working in the fields, and no one looked particularly sad which seemed strange. I thought we had come to the wrong place until I saw the simple wooden coffin in the centre.

It was also a little unsettling that there was no seating plan, just mats strewn around randomly. Relatives, friends and even strangers were left to sit or stand wherever they wanted. We weren't sure where we should position ourselves so we stood, waiting for the ceremony to begin. That's when my cousin, Leah, nudged me and said, "What about him, standing by the fence?"

I frowned at Leah's lack of respect for the dead, but I looked anyway and there, on the other side of the coffin, was Chuey. I shrugged, not really seeing why she would have thought it worth pointing out such an unremarkable young man.

"I don't know about the company he keeps though," snorted Leah. The ragged older man Chuey was talking with looked quite wild, with matted hair and clothes that appeared as though he had made them from animal skins and old sacks, even twigs and leaves.

My future husband didn't hold my attention for long. Leah had spotted the real reason we were attending the funeral. I turned to look, eager to see the boy who she had suddenly grown so keen on, but I was disappointed. He turned out to be thoroughly ordinary looking as well.

The ceremony was starting. There were still unoccupied mats, so we settled on the closest one. We were surprised to see that the funeral wasn't being led by holy men or scholars, but just by two friends of the dead man, and they were dressed as casually as anyone there. As they were about to begin, another cousin of ours arrived, Confucius.

Leah had told me that Cousin Confucius would be attending. She had mentioned it while trying to persuade me to accompany her, carefully letting the fact slip out in the way a fisherman drops a baited hook into a pool. I had once told her that I found our high-minded cousin attractive, even though he is a few years older, so she thought the news would change my mind and suddenly make me want to walk all the way to a funeral of a man I had never met. She was wrong. Any romantic ideas I might have once held about Confucius had cooled long before, mainly after he commented on my singing, saying that he 'preferred classical music to folk songs'. I had been quite wounded.

Leah's bait failed to tempt me, but the prospect of Confucius's attendance had more effect on my mother. "Oh, if Cousin Confucius will be there, then I suppose you may be permitted to go," she had said with a strange little smile, in a tone that I had learned not to argue with. So, in the end, Leah's angling had worked. With my parents forcing me along, her parents relented and she too was allowed to attend.

Confucius's arrival at the funeral caused quite a stir. We hadn't seen him for a couple of years as he had been away studying. His studies had transformed him. He was now wearing a long scholar's robe. It had the largest sleeves I had ever seen. He also wore a thin leather belt that somehow made him look as though his body was too long for his legs. Entering the gathering with arms held out slightly, Confucius slowly 'glided' in. The scholar's outfit was only part of his striking appearance. His face was hanging down in a look of pained grief, his head slightly tilted. The sorrow also appeared to affect the way he walked. It all seemed very odd as I had heard from Leah that Confucius barely knew the dead man.

It was a shock to see our cousin so altered and my heart sank for him, feeling that he was misjudging the tone of the ceremony. Leah's thoughts seemed less generous. She gasped and covered her face with her hands, turning towards me as though trying to hide. We watched as Confucius made a deep bow to the corpse before he crept slowly round to one of the last unoccupied mats on the other side of the coffin. The two friends of the dead man waited patiently while he carefully adjusted the position of the mat before kneeling down. They looked at him enquiringly as he arranged the skirts of his robe, both in front and behind. Eventually, he gravely nodded his head to show he was now ready, and the ceremony could finally proceed.

As the two friends began, it was clear that they were not following the usual order of service. Instead, they started by saying they wanted it to be a celebration of their friend's life. They then simply spoke of the times they had shared with the dead man and said how much they will miss him. I found their fond words moving, but they seemed to move Confucius quite differently. His grief-stricken look turned to a look of alarm. Leah and I, unlucky enough to be sitting opposite him, had nowhere else to look except at every scandalised twitch of our cousin's face.

During the ceremony, one of the friends reached behind the coffin and brought out a lute which he started to play, while the other friend sang a song they had composed. I had never heard of anyone singing at a funeral before, but it was a nice song asking 'where have you gone and why have you left us behind'. The look on Confucius's face turned to horror. In the middle of the song he stood up. Interrupting the singing, he demanded, "Might I enquire where you found this in the Rubrics for Obsequies?" He gestured towards the dead man, "Frivolous song-mongering in the presence of the departed!?" With that he stormed off, sleeves trailing.

The general murmur of amused astonishment allowed Leah and I to gasp out our own pent up laughter. I felt a pang of pity as I watched Cousin Confucius's angry exit, and a pang of guilt at our laughter, but then Leah and I looked at each other and laughed again.

As we tried to compose ourselves for the rest of the ceremony I noticed the reaction of the young man near the fence. He didn't seem as surprised as others. He shared a word with his companion and they both smiled. For some reason, I found myself smiling along with them.

After the ceremony, Leah immediately went over to speak to her lad. She introduced me briefly but I felt spare and awkward, not really part of their conversation. My attention wandered and, looking around, it settled on the young man Leah had pointed out and his wild looking friend. I watched them as they said their goodbyes, then I quickly had to turn my eyes away when he started walking straight towards us.

When Chuey arrived, it was obvious that he and Leah's lad knew each other well. Leah introduced us. From her slightly dramatic tone I realised that this was no chance encounter and that we were being set up. My first thought was about his name. 'Chewy?' I laughed to myself, thinking that some poor girl will end up marrying him and then she would be called 'Chewy's wife' for the rest of her days. That seemed quite unfortunate, but it didn't cross my mind that this would be my fate.

Neither Chuey nor I contributed much to the conversation, but when Leah spoke aghast at Confucius's conduct, Chuey gently excused him saying, "Ah well, perhaps he hasn't learned the new rites yet." I laughed out loud and our eyes met properly for the first time. It was quite a moment.

The mourners had nearly all left and the last few were already picking up the mats when Leah's young man gallantly suggested they escort us back to our village. Leah graciously accepted the offer and the four of us walked back together, Leah and her beau taking the lead, Chuey and I following behind.

We talked as we walked. I learned that his official name was Shaun but that everyone called him Chuey, that he was a fisherman and that he lived in one of the towns along the big river about half a day's travel away, and that he was staying with friends in the area.

"Like the man you were with at the funeral?" I asked.

"Yes", replied Chuey warmly, not seeming at all self-conscious about his strange looking friend.

Leah stopped us all a little way outside of our village. As we thanked the boys for seeing us home, Leah suggested that we all meet up again the following day. Leah's lad was keen and looked at Chuey for confirmation. Chuey was keen as well. Again our eyes met. I'm not sure I said anything intelligible, though I am sure my smile would have made any words unnecessary.

As we waved them off, Leah was clearly extremely pleased with herself. "Well I think that was a very good funeral, don't you Cousin?"

2. COURTING

Our courtship should have told me everything I needed to know about what it would be like being Chuey's wife. The day after the funeral, Leah and I set off from our village and met the lads as planned. I was surprised when, as soon as we'd met them, Leah suggested that we split up and all meet at the same spot later. With that, Leah and her young man went off together leaving Chuey and I alone to do whatever we wanted. That became our pattern for the next few weeks.

I don't know whether this dubious mutual chaperoning had been part of Leah's plan, but it certainly made courting very easy. It was a wonderfully free time, but Leah and I hadn't always enjoyed such freedom. It had come at a cost. Both of our fathers had lost their positions at court a few years earlier when they had fallen out of favour with a higher official. Swapping the comfort and expectations of court life for a poor rural existence had been hard on our families, but it did mean that us girls were mostly left to our own devices. Leah in particular, being a little older, looked for every opportunity to use this liberty to her advantage.

One time, after the four of us had met up at the end of a day, I was chatting with Leah. During a lull in our conversation, I overheard some of the lads' discussion. They were talking about the 'Tao'. It sounded a bit philosophical and not particularly interesting, but later, when I was alone with Leah, I asked her if she knew what 'Tao' was. Leah waved her hand dismissively. "Oh Tao, don't worry about it. It just means 'the way' or something." Then she leaned closer, as though about to tell a secret. "I will just say this Cousin, the wife and family of one who has the Tao will enjoy plenty, and live in comfort and happiness." She seemed to enjoy delivering this news.

I looked at her sideways. "And you think the boys have the Tao?" I queried, doubtfully.

Leah nodded very slowly, and very knowingly. "Yes, they do."

"What, Chuey too?" I laughed, unconvinced.

Her nodding continued, now in a more exaggerated fashion, with a smile on her lips as if to say, 'Now you understand, little cousin.' Seeing my continuing disbelief, she condescendingly ended the conversation with, "Oh well, don't worry. You can thank me later."

I didn't take Leah's claims about the boys' mysterious prospects seriously. Though she might pretend to have other motives, I knew she was desperately fond of her lad. I had certainly grown very keen on Chuey. I loved every minute of our time together. It was easy. It was fun. Conversation bubbled along and time flew. I only had one concern. Chuey was always great company and most attentive, but I found myself wondering whether anything was missing.

I had my reasons for caution. With my previous suitor, Sunny, it had all been so different. There was never any doubting Sunny's passion, but he had always seemed to be holding himself back. His inner conflict became more and more apparent until, finally, he told me that he thought that we should stop seeing each other. He said he was going to join the army and he felt that he could not be a good husband and a good soldier, and he didn't feel it would be fair to me for him to try to be both. "But I want to be a soldier's wife. I want to be *your* wife, Sunny," I had wept. I could see the pain in his face as he fought with the pull of his own emotions and I could see that he was quite overwhelmed as he turned and walked away. I was left devastated.

With Chuey it was nothing like that. It was all so easy, but even with all the laughter and the fun, I couldn't help asking myself whether I was just one of the friends that Chuey was visiting, like the wild man at the funeral. Perhaps one day he would say goodbye, in his friendly way, and I would never see him again. Those fears grew stronger after Leah and her lad set their wedding date. At first, I thought the news of Leah's engagement might help to move things on between us, but there was no change and I began to prepare myself for the worst.

Such was my fearful state of mind when Chuey picked his moment. I thought he had seemed a little quiet and thoughtful since we had met up that day. Some of the usual lightness was missing and I felt that he might have something on his mind. This carried on throughout the morning. My anxiety grew, feeling sure that I was heading towards the same painful outcome I had experienced with Sunny. This time I had seen it coming and I was determined to stay strong.

Then, while we were sitting in one of our favourite spots by the lake, Chuey started telling me about a dream he once had. In carefully chosen words he told me that he had dreamed that he was a butterfly. "In this dream, I was flitting around, enjoying myself. I was a butterfly. I had no idea I was Chuey." He told me this quite seriously, looking intensely into my face. He paused, then finished by saying, "The point is, ever since that dream, I can't be sure that it was really me, Chuey, who dreamed I was a butterfly, or whether I'm now really a sleeping butterfly dreaming that I'm Chuey."

He was searching my face, looking for some reaction or acknowledgement. He did not get one! I didn't know what to say, and I wasn't at all sure why he had felt the need to share this particular dream with me in such a dramatic fashion. Was it a joke? He certainly wasn't laughing. Was it supposed to be clever? He didn't seem to be waiting for applause. Then he asked, very seriously, if it bothered me, which seemed like a strange question.

"No", I answered, half laughing.

His face suddenly relaxed, filling with relief and happiness. He laughed, breathing out with the release, lying back with his arms out and looking up at the sky. Then he sat up, and that's when he asked if I thought we should get married. For some reason my own relief and happiness burst out as a flood of tears, but I managed to get "Yes, yes, yes" out between sobs as I threw my arms around his neck.

I thought my parents would be pleased to hear of our intentions. They had made it clear that they felt I was at an age when I should be married. A few weeks earlier, they had even invited the neighbours to our house for dinner, along with their third son. They had not warned me of the visit directly, but had suggested that I wear my best clothes for dinner.

The neighbours were farmers. When they arrived, it looked as though someone had tried to comb the third son's hair, somewhat unsuccessfully. It gave him a strange look that I instantly found disturbing. My parents tried their best to make small talk with their guests, but there is only so much conversation that can be had about the recent lack of rain. When the food was served, the third son immediately started shovelling rice into his mouth and had almost finished before the rest of us had started to eat. It hardly seemed real when I heard my parents, usually so mindful of polite manners, complimenting the guests on their son's healthy appetite. With his food finished, the third son started to look around the room, allowing himself occasional glances in my direction. I kept my eyes down. It had been an uncomfortable meal for all of us, but especially for me.

With my parents apparently so keen to be rid of me, I assumed they would welcome the news that Chuey and I wanted to get married. Instead, they reacted very coolly to the idea, saying they would need to 'consider' Chuey's proposal. It was a worrying time, particularly as I didn't understand my parents' reservations. Chuey was certainly nothing like Cousin Confucius, who they both continued to praise highly. Perhaps they weren't impressed that Chuey was only a fisherman, but at least in that line of work he should be able to feed us. I had overheard my mother refer to Leah's fiancé as a 'layabout'. Or was there something else about Chuey they disliked? Eventually, without further explanation, my parents informed me that they had decided to allow the marriage to proceed, though the funds they made available for the wedding would only allow a humble celebration.

I'm sure I'm not the only bride to have felt complicated emotions before their marriage, but an unexpected visit on the day before the wedding left me stunned. A smart young soldier came to our door, asking for me. He was carrying a large sack of rice. He politely informed me that Sunny would like me to accept it as a wedding present. I managed to politely thank him for delivering the rice and the young man went away. Back inside the house, I collapsed and wept uncontrollably, not even knowing why. It was an enormous gift for a newly enlisted soldier to give. That Sunny should have sent it to me left me barely able to breathe.

I had just about calmed down by the time Chuey arrived that evening. He had travelled back to his home town a few days earlier to make his own preparations for the start of our married life. When he returned he was driving a very smart carriage, with a spare horse tied behind. Going round to the back, he threw off a sheet to reveal two huge fish. He had also brought firewood, string, herbs and some big green leaves for cooking them. Also in the carriage was a large quantity of wine, a wedding gift from the man who had loaned him the carriage. Everyone was very impressed.

With the rice Sunny had given us and the fish and wine that Chuey had brought, suddenly we had enough for a feast. Extra invitations were hurriedly sent out.

The wedding day went well. As the party progressed, it was hard not to notice the behaviour of the neighbours' third son, who was becoming rather loud and unpleasant, his rustic humour loosened by the large amount of wine he was gulping. I looked over and smiled at Chuey, feeling very lucky and relieved that I was now his wife and not the wife of the farmer's third son.

3. MARRIED

Perhaps no one really knows who they are marrying until after the wedding. I certainly learned a lot about Chuey in the first few days of our marriage. Looking back, I suppose that started as soon as we were leaving the ceremony. We left much later than planned. Chuey had seemed relaxed, even as I lingered over each goodbye, including a very fond and emotional farewell with my parents. There were some tears, but all of them were good tears. After Chuey had finished arranging my things in the carriage, I was surprised to see that he carefully placed his sword on top of the luggage and covered it with a blanket, leaving just the handle showing.

We had kept up a good pace, swapping the horses regularly, but we were still quite a way from Chuey's town when the light started to fade. Chuey became quieter and, I sensed, more alert as we drove through the dusk. A couple of times he pulled the horse to a stop and peered into the gloom, his hand reaching for the sword, before gently coaxing the horse to move on. I was starting to regret our delayed departure, but when we came to the first houses on the outskirts of the town Chuey seemed to relax again.

I couldn't make out much detail as we drove through the town but I could see the walls getting taller. Then I saw great tiled roofs rising behind the walls, the outlines of their elegant curves making daunting shapes against the fading light of the sky. After passing an inn we soon left the buildings behind and were driving through countryside once more.

The darkness was almost complete and the horse was getting skittish and difficult to control by the time Chuey slowed the carriage to a near halt before turning hard towards the black mass of mountains rising to the left. I could feel that the track was very uneven and there were few houses. It seemed the blackness of the mountains almost filled the sky by the time we arrived at the house that was to be my home. Chuey was surprised to see light coming from behind the shutters. When he opened the door we were met by the warmth of a fire, which had obviously been well tended until shortly before our arrival. A supper of chicken soup and steamed buns had been anonymously left warming to welcome us.

Chuey went out to unharness and feed the horses and I took my first look around my new home. Chuey had been right, the house was small and very basic. It even had a central hearth, but it was cosy and even from those first moments it felt like home. It's funny to remember now but what delighted me most was that there was no smell of fish. That had been one of my main fears when imagining what life as a fisherman's wife might be like.

My first full day as a married woman was lovely enough. I remember waking up with a strange sense of freedom. I sat up and looked around the small empty house and laughed to myself as I wondered what it might have looked like before Chuey had returned to get things ready for my arrival. Chuey was already making up the fire and preparing to heat up some of the food we had brought from the wedding. He said he was going outside to fetch water, so I wrapped a blanket around my shoulders and followed, keen to see where I was now living.

Stepping outside into the fresh clear morning, I stopped, my mouth open. Chuey noticed my awestruck expression and smiled. Mountains rose steeply on three sides of the wide valley. The foreboding black shapes of the night before, now backed by blue sky and white clouds, held a serene beauty, like statues of ancient kings standing guard over our home. I could see a few houses dotted down the lane back towards the main road, but up the valley there was nothing apart from an area of derelict terracing where a smaller valley went off to the left.

I soon got to know who had left such a warm welcome for us on our wedding night. We had been out for the morning, in the carriage. Chuey had suggested that we use it to go for a picnic as we needed to return it to its owner the following day. After driving to the market for provisions, we had driven back past the end of our lane and on to a spot overlooking the place where two rivers meet. The smaller river was itself bigger than any near my village, but the big river was stunningly wide, the far bank so distant that you couldn't tell an ox from a horse. Together, enjoying our feast while looking out over the vast expanse of flowing water, I felt that we could have been the king and queen of the whole world. It was just the sort of experience you would wish for any newlywed couple.

After the picnic and our outdoor siesta, driving home, Chuey pulled the carriage to a stop outside the house closest to ours. He shouted out a greeting as he jumped down and went to the back of the carriage to collect the bowls, plates and spoons from the night before. A woman came out of the door wiping her hands on a cloth. When she saw me she beamed me a big smile. Chuey said, "I don't suppose you know who these belong to, do you?" though it was clear that he had already guessed. She ignored Chuey's question and came straight over to introduce herself.

"Hello, I'm Sue. How was the soup? Was it alright?" then she asked how I was finding married life and welcomed me to the neighbourhood. I thanked her for such a wonderfully welcoming and thoughtful wedding present.

It had been a blissful start to married life, but perhaps life isn't meant to run that smoothly. It started the next day, when Sue asked me an unsettling question while we were coming back from doing our washing. Sue had woken us that morning when she had knocked on our door and called out, asking if I wanted to go with her to do the washing. I looked at Chuey. He seemed encouraging, saying he would have to go out to check the fish traps anyway, so I had shouted out, "Yes, thanks Sue, I'll be right out". I frantically dressed myself while grabbing a few items of clothing to wash, including some very fishy trousers I found outside the back door.

As we set off down the lane with our bundles of dirty clothes, Sue explained that she wouldn't have disturbed us so early but that she always did her washing on the fifth day of the week, adding that I'd soon get used to the routine. She stopped suddenly, gasped and seemed quite worried. "I forgot to tell you! Oh dear, I should have told you already!" Then she explained that it was important that we don't do any washing in the stream near our houses as that was the source of the town's drinking water. "But," she said with a big smile, "we can use the slabs in the town square."

I must have seemed less than enthusiastic at having to walk such a long way to wash clothes.

"It's not far," she said brightly. "There's a short cut!" She added that it's a lot easier to walk to the nice clean slabs rather than trying to wash clothes in the stream. "And you'll like the women. They're a good bunch on the fifth day. Not as snooty as earlier in the week."

The short cut brought us out next to the town square. I had seen it the day before. It wasn't really a square, just a very wide stretch of road, with government buildings along one side and businesses along the far side. As we crossed the road, I could see two neat lines of slabs flanking a stream that emerged from under the road opposite the fountain that was the town's main water supply.

Sue dropped her washing down onto the first of a pair of adjacent free slabs, announcing to all that I was Chuey's new wife. After a brief welcome the women returned to their gossip about some local infidelity.

There seemed to be a hierarchy in the positioning on the slabs. The loudest woman occupied the first slab, closest to the road. Sue and I were towards the far end, between the inn and some sort of clothes emporium. I missed most of what the women were saying, but I didn't mind. I was more interested in overhearing the conversation of a group of lads who were sitting at a table outside the inn. They were discussing the existence of ghosts. I couldn't imagine any of the lads from my village having such a serious debate, which left me wondering how I would ever fit in with this sophisticated town life.

Even with the time it took to work the dried fish slime and scales out of Chuey's trousers, I had soon finished washing our few items. I continued to rinse and re-rinse them, my fingers aching from the freezing mountain water, until Sue announced that she had finished too.

It was then, while we walked back, that Sue asked, "So, what made you want to marry our Chuey?" It was just a pleasant, light question, but I didn't have an answer.

"I, um, er, I um …," I stammered, shaking my head, unable to form any ideas or words.

Sue tried to help me, "I just mean, an attractive girl like you, I'm sure you could have had the pick of the local lads."

I tried to come up with an answer, but still I couldn't find a single word. Sue took my awkward struggling look as a question, which she then tried to answer.

"Well, I just mean, well, he's a bit …," she paused, then laughed, "well, he's a bit unusual, isn't he!"

I still had no words to offer, and looked forward as we walked on.

Sue broke the awkward silence. "Sorry, I shouldn't have pried. I'm sure you've got your own very good reasons. And don't worry. We all like Chuey. I'm just glad that you're so, er, ordinary. None of us were quite sure what Chuey would be coming home with!" Sue had clearly meant this as a compliment and something of a joke. In truth, I suppose I had always thought of myself as fairly ordinary but I didn't enjoy hearing that my new next-door neighbour agreed.

My wounded expression prompted Sue to try again. "Sorry, I don't seem to be able to say anything right today. No, I just meant that you're probably just what Chuey needs to sort himself out: a good down-to-earth young woman like yourself." She could see that her attempt to undo the affront had made matters even worse, with my puzzled expression asking, 'Why would Chuey need to sort himself out?'

The silence continued for a moment longer, with Sue probably rather wondering why Chuey had chosen to marry me. Then she asked about my family and the conversation continued on safer ground.

Arriving back at our house I paused, almost feeling that I should knock. I didn't. Chuey was still out. Once inside, I found myself looking around at my new home. Why had I come to live there?

When Chuey returned, he seemed pleased with himself. He had already traded his catch and was carrying a small sack of millet and some vegetables as well as some small fish on a loop of string. After Sue's awkward question, I found myself looking at him afresh. Chuey turned around and caught me mid-stare. There was a slightly awkward moment but it was soon laughed off.

Sue's question, and my failure to answer, had been uncomfortable but at the time the question itself didn't trouble me too much. Chuey was lovely and maybe that was enough. However, her question, and her mention of his 'strangeness', did plant a seed in my mind. It grew later that day when I came to see some of Chuey's strangeness for myself when we returned the carriage and horses to his friend, Hue.

Before we left, Chuey had asked if I would mind if we visited another friend as part of the trip. The friend was sick and Chuey thought he might welcome some company and a meal. I agreed that it was a nice idea, so we took some food with us when we set off to return the carriage. First we called at Hue's house and I realised that all three of us would be making the trip to see the sick man.

Chuey had said I would like Hue and he was right. He was a little older than Chuey. After Chuey had introduced us, I thanked Hue for the loan of the carriage and then tried to explain how important his gift of wine had been for the wedding, but my speech was starting to sound laboured. Hue immediately helped me out, waving away my explanation, saying he was pleased the wine had been useful and adding that he was just sorry that he hadn't been able to attend in person.

The sick man was asleep when we arrived. He awoke as we entered and tried to get up to welcome us. The first thing I noticed was the terrible ulcer on his head. Chuey and Hue insisted that he stayed under his warm covers. Even then, I could see that his body was unnaturally twisted. Chuey jovially introduced me as his new wife. As I approached him I was struck by an unpleasant smell, something between sweet rotten apples and old meat. I tried not to breathe in, hoping my revulsion was not apparent.

The man was clearly in a great deal of pain, but he didn't make much of it. In fact he seemed to be in remarkably good spirits as he wished us well in our married life. Chuey and Hue kept up a friendly chat, but it struck me as odd that the three men should laugh and joke as though nothing was wrong. Even when the conversation turned to the man's illness the tone was just as light-hearted. The sick man's jokes about his body would have been in extremely poor taste had they come from anyone's mouth but his own. He pointed to an unpleasant growth on his arm, saying, "And now this tree has decided to start growing out of my elbow!"

Chuey mentioned the food we had brought and I was glad to be able to busy myself tending the fire. While I heated the soup I listened, amazed that the laughter continued, mixed with the sound of wheezing, coughing and gasps of pain.

When the soup had warmed, I brought over a bowlful. It became obvious that the sick man could not manage the spoon for himself, so Chuey helped him. The man was giving me a grin of appreciation when a sudden spasm sent the bowl flying, showering Chuey with soup. Chuey's surprised yelp showed he wasn't badly scolded and, while he wiped his clothes, I fetched another bowlful to resume the feeding.

As I spooned soup into the man's eager mouth I couldn't understand how he could be so unmoved by his plight, but my frown of pity was met by his open smile. When the soup was finished my curiosity overcame my politeness. As I wiped his face I asked whether he was alright.

"Oh yes" he laughed, looking straight into my eyes with a twinkle in his own. "If the Great Maker wants my elbow for a tree, what is it to me? And if my buttocks want to turn into wheels, well then my spirit can become a horse and I'll ride around in my own wagon! Why should I mind?" I forced a smile, nodding in admiration at his positive attitude to such terrible suffering.

Chuey asked his sick friend whether he would like one of us to stay, but he waved the offer away. He seemed to genuinely prefer us not make such a fuss and looked quite jolly as we closed the door behind ourselves.

On the way home, Chuey and Hue carried on their conversation in as light a manner as they had with their sick friend. I kept quiet. It disturbed me that they seemed to have no concern for their friend's pitiful state. I sat quietly next to Chuey as the two men merrily discussed the nature of the changes that human beings undergo. I had been experiencing a lot of change in my own life, but I didn't join the discussion. My thoughts were still with the dying man we had left alone.

After Hue had dropped us off, I was still lost in thought. Sue was right. Chuey was unusual. I had seen that now and it left me with a strange, uneasy feeling.

A few nights later I would get another insight into my husband's strange ways. Again, Hue was involved. He was a frequent and welcome visitor to our home, often coming for dinner and staying to talk well into the evening. More often than not the conversation would become some sort of duel of words. I often saw Chuey practicing with his sword and I had heard he was a good swordsman, but with Hue it was the cut and thrust of ideas. Perhaps, instead of fencing, their conversations sometimes seemed more like wrestling. They writhed and grappled before Chuey invariably delivered the final throw. Hue would be left bloodied but unbowed, laughing with frustration and promising to set Chuey straight the next time he called. By then Chuey would have subtly reworded his position and Hue would be left chasing his shadows again. I enjoyed listening to their bouts and would quietly occupy myself with some household task while they tussled.

On this particular night, dinner had been cleared away and Chuey and Hue were getting into a deep discussion. As I returned from rinsing the dishes, I could hear that Hue's voice was full of determined excitement. He leaned forward, pointing at Chuey, as though he were about to deliver the final victorious blow. I smiled to myself as I sat down and began spinning.

Hue was adamant, insisting "No, that is a silly idea. No one can be without emotions."

"Yes, they can."

"Look, Chuey, emotions are the essentials of man, agreed? Logically that means that if anyone has no emotions they have ceased to be a man. So, no one can be a man and be without emotions. You can't get out of that one." Hue sat back chuckling, with his arms crossed and a self-satisfied, victorious look on his face. But Chuey was smiling as well.

"No my friend. The Tao gives him a face and Heaven gives him a shape, how can he not be called a man?"

"Exactly! He is called a man! Precisely my point. How can he be called a man if he is without the essentials of man! Ah ha! Got you!"

"When I say 'without emotions' I mean someone who does not allow either the good or the bad to have any effect on them. Judging 'good' or 'bad', or 'better' or 'worse', taking sides, loving and hating, is not what I mean by a man's essentials. Such views can only inwardly wound his person and obscure his true vision. The true man does not indulge in these futile and damaging exercises. He has no fixed judgements applying to all circumstances. He sees and knows, in the moment."

The debate rumbled on, with them defining and re-defining the essentials of man. By the time Hue left, I would have judged Chuey to have been the marginal winner, but that night my thoughts were not on the contest.

I had been sitting there with only half an ear on the ever subtler definition of the 'essentials of man'. I had been thinking about something Chuey had said earlier on. He had said that the 'true man' doesn't love or hate. He had said it in passing, quite lightly, but I had heard it clearly enough. If Chuey thinks that the ideal man shouldn't be loving or hating it raised some worrying questions for me, his wife. Perhaps I should have joined in the debate, challenging my husband on being loveless, but instead I carried on spinning in silence.

As we were going to sleep that night Chuey said that he pitied Hue, wearing himself out with his petty arguments about words and their meanings. He said Hue was like someone who tries to have the last word with an echo. I probably mumbled something in reply but I could not wholeheartedly agree with my husband. Hue's probing had uncovered something real. Hearing that Chuey's ideal man does not love brought back all the fears from our courtship and the concern raised by the trip to see Chuey's dying friend. I suddenly felt very vulnerable and a long way from home.

4. VISITORS

I didn't sleep well after hearing that Chuey thought that a true man does not love, but the next morning Chuey was his usual loving self and my fears receded like a bad dream. This, however, was a bad dream that stayed somewhere in the back of my mind. Most of the time those feelings of insecurity were just a distant, hazy memory. I came to view Chuey's 'philosophising' as just a game he played. And there was plenty of philosophising at our house. Visitors came from near and far, arriving with no purpose other than to discuss things with Chuey. I often wondered why they came to consult a simple fisherman, though I suppose I always knew that there was nothing simple about Chuey, except for his wife perhaps.

I was still curious about the mysterious Tao, and my interest would rise whenever it was mentioned. None of my eavesdropping yielded much insight. The times I overheard it being discussed usually left me even more puzzled than before. I thought I might get some answers when a portly scholar arrived one day, saying he had come particularly to enquire about the Tao. I had been putting the washing out to dry when he arrived so I called to Chuey and made sure I stayed close enough to hear their conversation.

As soon as Chuey appeared at the door, the scholar, without waiting to be invited in, started his questioning saying he was keen to know *where* the Tao is.

Chuey looked surprised at the question. Stepping outside to join his visitor, Chuey waved his hand around and said, "Well, it's everywhere." But that didn't satisfy the man who wanted something more concrete. Chuey obliged. "Well, it's in this ant," he said, putting his hand in the path of an ant who climbed onto his palm before walking round to the back of his hand, causing Chuey to twist his arm round as he kept it in view.

"Is that its lowest point?" asked the visitor.

"Well, it's in this grass" said Chuey, trying to encourage the ant to continue its travels onto the blade of grass, which it eventually did.

"Fascinating. And is that its lowest point?"

Chuey kicked a bit of broken tile with his toe. "It's in this tile"

"And that, I think, must be its lowest point?" ventured the man.

"Well, it is in piss and shit as well, but I think your questions miss the point. After all, if it wasn't in piss and shit it would hardly be fit to be called the Great Tao now would it?"

The visitor seemed startled at that, as I was myself. He promptly brought the audience to a close, thanking Chuey for his time and returning to his carriage. There was a certain amount of haughtiness as he bid us, "Good day," but Chuey didn't seem at all bothered.

Even if my attempts to understand the Tao proved disappointing, I still enjoyed my husband's performance in the debates. Try as they might, the visitors never defeated him. Whenever they attempted to trap Chuey in a strangle-hold of logic, he simply started talking illogically to free himself. A scholar once asked him about happiness and how to attain it. Chuey said that you don't find it till you stop looking for it, leaving the puzzled scholar at a loss for words. I had never seen Chuey at a loss for words so I asked him once if he had ever been beaten.

"Beaten?" he laughed, amused that I saw it as a competition. "Oh yes", he said, clearly enjoying the chance to recount his defeat. "Yes, I was once soundly beaten. I saw a skull lying by the road one day. I tapped it with my rod and asked what had brought it to such a state. I asked whether he had succumbed to an attack by some bandit, or whether he had died in war. Or had bad behaviour or poverty been the cause? Or had death come naturally at the end of a full and long life? Then I picked up the skull and used it as a pillow." I gasped at Chuey's irreverence but he carried on unconcerned.

"In the middle of the night the skull came to me in a dream and put me in my place. He said that after death there are neither superiors or inferiors, no seasons nor work. He said the peace surpasses the happiness of kings. At first I didn't believe the skull, challenging him, saying 'If I could get the Ruler of our Destiny to restore your body to life with its bones and flesh and skin, and to give you back your father and mother, your wife and children, and all your village acquaintances, would you wish me to do so?' The skull stared at me and said, 'Why should I cast away my royal peace just to undertake again the toils of life among mankind?'" Chuey said he had been quite beaten as I had called it, and added that the biggest lesson the skull had given him was to be wary of gabbling on like a public speaker, talking about things he didn't know about.

I had asked Chuey a reasonable question, but he used one of his silly stories to turn it all upside down and back the same way again, leaving me with no answer at all but, at the same time, with an answer of sorts. I could see why people sometimes became frustrated in their discussions with him.

Chuey placed no value on his skill. He said that just because someone gets the better of someone in a duel with swords, it doesn't mean they are any more right, and if someone gets the better of someone in a duel with words, it still doesn't necessarily follow that they are any more right. Even though Chuey dismissed his skills, I loved to hear his dance of words.

I soon grew more relaxed about the constant stream of visitors and gave up trying to quickly tidy the house each time I heard a carriage arriving. Then one evening, two men arrived at our door. One of the men was middle-aged and his younger companion seemed to be a similar age to Chuey. Both were very well dressed. The younger man said they were staying overnight in the town to break their journey.

We had already eaten our dinner and I had nothing to offer the guests except some sweet brittle-cakes that I had accidentally burnt almost to a cinder. While Chuey was arranging cushions around the fire, I attracted his attention and discreetly pointed to the cakes to see whether he thought I should offer them to the guests. Chuey shrugged as if to say 'why not', so I tried to find a clean plate on which to present my charred offering.

While the three of them debated, I carried on with my spinning. As usual, Chuey was running humorous rings round the guests' serious questions. At the end of the evening, the two men left after politely thanking me for my hospitality, which Chuey and I had a good laugh about once they had gone. I found one of the cakes while clearing out the ashes the next day. I don't know what happened to the other one.

The next morning I was in the middle of doing my washing, at my usual slab next to Sue, when the two guests from the night before came out of the inn. They sat at one of the tables to take their tea in the morning sun while their carriage was made ready. I kept my face down, though I suppose there would have been little chance of them recognising the mouse-like wife from the night before. I cringed when they started talking about their visit to our house. Thankfully the brittle-cakes weren't mentioned, but they did talk a lot about Chuey.

The younger man seemed very pensive. He said he had studied the ways of the sage-kings, all manner of other subjects and that he had gained a firm grasp of the hundred schools of thought. He then said, "And now I hear the words of this man, Chuey, and I am disturbed by them." He looked at his companion and asked, "Why is that? Does he know more than I, or is his understanding better than mine?"

The older man leaned forward and sighed heavily. He smiled and said, "Have you heard about the frog in the well?"

"No," said the younger man.

The older man laughed and said in a kindly fashion, "Let me tell you about the frog in the broken-down old well." He then went on to compare his well-educated companion to a frog who was very happy with his dirty old well. Then he compared Chuey to the great turtle of the North Sea. He said that the younger man's knowledge and understanding amounted to a stagnant puddle compared to Chuey's far-reaching insight. He finished by telling him to forget trying to understand Chuey's words as that would be like a mosquito trying to carry a mountain on his back. It would only make him forget all of his own little knowledge. The younger man bore the chastening words with fortitude and even thanked his companion for them.

During this exchange I could feel my cheeks burning as I stared down at my washing. Sue looked at me and raised her eyebrows in an exaggerated fashion and said, "Well!" I wasn't sure whether she meant it as a joke.

I was already struggling to cope with the conversation I had just overheard when a neatly dressed coachman approached the two men. I didn't catch the coachman's question but I heard the younger man's reply. "No, that won't be necessary. I'll travel with the Duke."

I almost gasped out loud. A duke had been sitting in our tiny, cluttered cottage. Now this member of the nobility was sat here praising Chuey. I winced as I remembered the brittle-cakes and could hardly breathe.

The visit of the Duke and his younger companion filled my mind for a long time. Perhaps Leah's claim that 'the wife and family of one who has the Tao will enjoy plenty and live in comfort' wasn't so far-fetched after all.

5. A VISITOR

Being away from my home village, away from everyone I knew, was harder than I might have admitted, even to myself. In the market, I'd spot faces I thought I recognised, only to realise that they weren't the actual people, just something deep inside of me yearning for someone familiar. But one day I did see a familiar face, and it was a bit of a shock.

I heard a carriage draw up and went to the door. On opening it, I found Cousin Confucius standing there. "Ah, esteemed Cousin", he greeted me bowing deeply, "I have come to pay a visit on you and your new husband, if that might be acceptable." Confucius was wearing the same scholar's robe he had been wearing at the funeral. A boy wearing a similar robe was unhitching the horse.

Seeing a piece of my past suddenly appear in my new world left me momentarily speechless, but politeness has always been a deep instinct in my family. I stepped back and opened the door wider to welcome my cousin in, saying, "Oh Cousin, what a nice surprise."

As Confucius and his young companion entered our humble cottage I was painfully aware of the jumble lying around, imagining what my cousin might be thinking of the mess. Confucius gave no sign of any ill impression. I offered tea to the guests, starting to enjoy the honour of my cousin's visit and the unexpected chance to show off my new status. Confucius introduced the young student as Yan and said that they were travelling to the capital where he hoped to be granted an audience with the king.

Confucius asked where they should put their things, and that was the first indication that they wanted to stay the night. That threw me into some confusion. The cottage was a comfortable size for two, but even in those days it could feel cramped, filled with Chuey's fishing tackle and hunting equipment. I didn't feel I could offer to put up my cousin and his pupil for the night without checking with Chuey, but he had gone off with his fishing partner, Euan, and I wasn't expecting him back for a while.

At my hesitation, Confucius took charge of the situation. "It's alright, here will be fine," he said, moving some fishing rods and putting his pack in the corner. Then, in the direction of Yan he said in a scholarly voice, "Even with just an arm for a pillow, a scholar can still have joy." Turning to me he said, "We'll be no trouble. Here, we have brought provisions." And with that he handed me a very small bag of rice. I remember thinking, 'Well, that won't go far!' But I thanked him anyway.

My honour at Confucius's visit didn't last long. As soon as he had finished his tea Confucius stood up and announced that he would head off up the road now, then asked whether it would be alright for Yan to stay behind. Despite my reservations, the words 'yes, of course' came out of my mouth as yet another involuntary polite reaction.

Confucius left and I sat there with Yan, a little awkwardly, not sure what to say. Curiosity got the better of me and I went to the door to see where Confucius was going. I was surprised to see that, yes, he was heading up the valley. I was about to call out to him that there was nothing further up the lane and that the town was in the other direction, but then decided that he could find out his mistake for himself.

I paused in the doorway. I looked at Yan and Yan smiled back at me. The silence continued. I breathed in to say something, thought of nothing and breathed out, but then Yan said brightly, "The master has been greatly looking forward to visiting the old man."

"Oh," I said, somewhat surprised.

After a while I asked whether Yan was alright, just sitting there. "Oh yes," he said, and seemed genuinely content, like a puppy waiting for his master to return.

"Right, well, I'll just get on with, er, some spinning then."

Yan smiled back, apparently feeling a whole lot more comfortable with the situation than I was.

It was a relief when Chuey and Euan returned for lunch. "Oh, who's this?" said Chuey as a friendly welcome when he saw Yan. I hurriedly explained that Confucius had arrived and this was Yan, and would it be alright if they stayed the night. Chuey seemed perfectly happy with all of that and went out the back with Euan to clean their catch.

I followed them outside and whispered to Chuey, "Confucius went off, walking up the lane towards the hills, apparently to see an old man."

"Oh," was his unconcerned answer.

"I didn't know that anyone lived further up."

"Oh yes, the old man, in the upper valley."

"Oh," I said, and went back inside to see if the beans were ready, feeling somehow a little hurt and annoyed that my cousin seemed to know more about my neighbours than I did.

As we sat eating lunch, Yan asked in his wide-eyed, open and interested way, "Did you catch any?"

"Yes. Not a bad morning," replied Chuey, taking a mouthful of bean cake.

"Did you use a single hook or a gang of hooks?" continued Yan, quickly adding, "My master only ever uses a single hook." The comment hadn't been a challenge, but I guess we all felt the edge implied.

Chuey and Euan exchanged a little look. Euan answered flatly, "Spear." Many evenings at our fireside had taught me that under his softly-spoken manner Euan had a dry sense of humour. I brought my hand up to my mouth to hide a growing smile.

"Oh," said Yan, not quite sure what to make of the unexpected reply. Chuey and Euan shared another look, still somehow managing to keep straight faces, though I noticed that Chuey was smiling too as he took his next mouthful.

Yan stood watching me as I prepared dinner, which I found rather disturbing. I didn't like having an audience but he had failed to take any of my hints that he might like to go and do something else. Chuey had been right, it had been a good morning, and the house was full of the smell of a meaty pot of turtle stew by the time Confucius returned. Chuey and Euan were drinking and chatting by the fire. Confucius immediately started honouring his 'munificent host'. To me he just said, "Good evening Cousin." I thought he seemed a little depressed.

Yan was keen for news. "Master, might I enquire how your audience with the old man went? Did he give you a lesson?"

With a slightly puzzled look Confucius said, "Yes, I think so. Yes, I suppose he did, sort of."

I was listening for a fuller report but Confucius didn't seem to be feeling very talkative and the conversation moved on. After a while, Euan stood up and said that he was leaving. Chuey protested and managed to persuade his friend to stay for the meal.

Everyone was impressed by the turtle stew. Even with Confucius's and Yan's impressive appetites there was still plenty left at the end, which was good because shortly after we finished eating, Joe arrived bearing a jar of his latest batch of apple wine.

I had first seen Joe when he had walked past one time while Sue and I had been doing our washing. He was obviously quite a character so I had asked Sue who he was. "Mad Joe. Town nutter. Harmless," had been her dismissive reply. Harmless or not, I remember being quite startled by his "Helloo" the first time that his mad-looking eyes, framed by his wild hair and wild beard, appeared around our door. Since then Joe had become a regular visitor, his merry wit livening up many evenings at our house.

It was quite a party as we sat round the fire after dinner. I started to relax into my role as hostess, even imagining the good report Confucius would be passing on to my mother. First the conversation centred on the day's hunting, including Yan telling Confucius that they had used spears to catch the turtles. Chuey explained why spears are better for turtles. Confucius nodded politely, but I didn't get the impression he was about to start using spears himself. From there the conversation moved on to the turtle stew and other recipes.

The tone changed slightly when Joe said that he had noticed Confucius's scholar's gown, which was hardly much of a claim, and asked him what he studied. Confucius adopted his scholarly voice and said, "Primarily the paths trodden by the sage-kings of old."

Then Yan added keenly, "The master knows all the six classics," and looked at his master for praise. He was rewarded with a little smile, though I thought it looked a little forced. Yan didn't seem to notice. He was beaming as brightly and as openly as ever.

Joe continued his questioning. "So, what is it that you find worth learning in all those dusty old books?"

"Generally, it is the application of benevolence and righteousness to the governing of a province." I had the impression that Confucius was feeling a little uneasy at the turn the conversation had taken.

"Oh, so you have land you govern, eh?" asked Joe.

"Er, no."

"Oh, so you must be an advisor to a king then?" Joe thrust his head forward in an impish manner.

Confucius was floundering. "Er no, but I am on my way to …"

"So you're not a ruler, nor even an advisor to a ruler." Joe paused, then said, "Well, do you have any job?" Not waiting for a reply, he stood up with his eyes rolling and arms waving and gave his pronouncement. "This man is wearing out his body and exhausting his heart with no good reason to. And they call me mad! I believe that if he carries on like this he will be putting his true nature in danger!"

To those of us used to Joe's extravagant gestures this was a common display, but it must have been alarming for Confucius and Yan.

Next, Euan looked up from the fire, where he was using the poker to rearrange the logs. "So, what was it you felt the need to consult the old man about earlier?"

Confucius looked a little hounded. "I was asking him why I had not had much success in putting my knowledge of the ways of benevolence and righteousness into practice."

Euan carefully placed a log on the fire and watched it as it began to catch alight. Without looking up he continued, "And, did he tell you why?"

Confucius glumly related that the old man had told him that he had been fortunate that no ruler had agreed to govern his country in that way. Euan looked round at Chuey.

Chuey was nodding slowly in agreement as he watched the sparks rising from the fire as the new wood crackled. He said quietly, "Ever since the sage-kings first taught benevolence and righteousness, all under heaven has been troubled and distorted by their teaching, as everything rushes around trying to live up to it."

Yan looked questioningly at his master, obviously expecting a forthright response. His look turned to confusion as Confucius merely sat there, staring into the fire.

Joe still had a glint in his eye and I thought he might be about to renew his attack, so I said, "Joe! How about a song, to liven things up a bit?" Everyone thought that was a good idea and Joe stood up to deliver one of his songs. I didn't expect that it would be to Confucius's tastes, but I guessed it would have been better than the conversation which might have otherwise developed. Perhaps I shouldn't have bothered.

Joe sang his song and Confucius politely complimented him on it, prompting Joe to invite him to join in. "If you would sing it once more I will be delighted to sing along with the third chorus," said Confucius in a friendly tone.

I was pleased that the singing had brought a lighter mood, but then Yan spoke again. "When the master hears a piece he likes he always asks the singer to sing it a second time before joining in." Again he beamed at Confucius, looking for his reward. This time the little smile that Confucius granted him was even more pained.

I think it was Euan who first gave a snort of laughter. Yan, bewildered by the reaction to his contribution to the conversation, innocently asked, "What's funny?" which didn't help at all.

Confucius adopted a serious expression and said solemnly, "Personally, I have never found it difficult to hold my wine."

Just as at the funeral where I had first met Chuey, I bit my lip, feeling for my cousin and his rigid ways. Euan seemed to be struggling to contain his mirth as he stood up saying, "I'm going to have to go. See you all," and quickly left. Joe was shaking his head, openly chuckling to himself. He said that he too should be heading off.

It had been an awkward end to the evening. As I arranged the mats for sleeping, it struck me that if I had been more inclined to follow my mother's wishes, I might have been placing my mat next to Confucius's mat rather than next to Chuey's. The idea made me laugh, but then the smile quickly disappeared as I thought about how different my life could have been.

At breakfast I was trying especially hard to be an attentive host. Then I picked a quiet moment to try to explain to Confucius that Joe and Euan might have strange ideas and ways but that they weren't being malicious. Confucius didn't seem to be bearing any grudges about the previous night's laughter at his expense. I very tactfully tried to suggest that it was maybe a bit like the funeral, when he had stormed off because of the singing, and that he might want to consider, sometimes, whether it wasn't better just to go with the flow, perhaps just a bit now and then.

"I know. I know," he said. "These people go beyond the human world, while I am condemned by heaven to travel within the human world. That within and that beyond can't really ever mix. I know that. I know."

I said I didn't feel it was quite as stark as that and maybe he could just lighten up a bit. Confucius seemed almost offended. "But if a scholar is not grave, how will he call forth any veneration? What ruler would employ such a man?"

Sometimes my cousin could be so infuriating! I wanted to say that there hadn't actually been any rulers around our fire the night before, and perhaps lightening up would have been alright. I somehow managed to swallow that annoyed little thought. Instead, I calmly tried to suggest that I felt he was being rather ambitious in trying for a career in government. I dared to point out that he didn't actually have any experience, whereas the government officials were trained professionals. Confucius laughed at the thought, saying that the people currently involved in public life were all "puny vessels with hardly any capacity," adding dismissively, "Huh, they don't count." Then he looked at me very intensely and said, "Oh Cousin, if any ruler were to employ me, in a year I could make a difference, in three years the government would be perfected."

I looked at my cousin, so keen to put the world right. My heart went out to him and I would have dearly loved to have been able to say the right thing, to help him, but I don't suppose that was ever going to happen. Another time, I overheard him telling Yan that, "Girls and servants are particularly hard to manage." I don't know whether he saw me as more of a girl or as more of a servant, but either way it was clear that nothing I could say would be of any help at all, so I just smiled.

I heard Sue calling to me from outside. I had forgotten it was the fifth day. I shouted to her to save me a slab. When I arrived in the square Sue wasted no time in letting me know that she had noticed Confucius's arrival. "So, you've started a school now have you? I see the scholars have moved in."

I explained that Confucius was a distant cousin, and that he was just stopping for the night on his way to the capital. I must have said that during a lull in the chatter because one of the other women shouted, "If that's her cousin, it's no wonder she married Chuey!" They all thought that was very funny, though I couldn't see any connection. I kept my resentment to myself.

When the group chatter had moved on to some other victim I quietly asked Sue about the old man who Confucius had been visiting. Surprisingly, she hadn't known that anyone lived further up our lane either, but she didn't feel the need to keep the matter private, saying in a loud voice, "Lily will know," adding even louder, "Yes, there aren't many men round these parts that Lily doesn't know." Lily was the stout woman who always occupied the first slab. I envied Sue's confidence.

"I heard that!" came the invited response, but the affronted manner was clearly not meant to fool anyone. "Anyway, what man will I know?"

Sue repeated my question, asking about the old man further up our road.

"Oh, I didn't know he was still alive." Lily went on to tell us that her mother had told her that he had been an old man even when she had been a girl. "And I'll tell you something else." Lily paused so that we could ready ourselves for the revelation. "He was in his mum's tummy for 72 years before he was born. Yes, that's right, he was 72 years old when he was born! And he already had his long ears even then."

Everyone laughed. But Lily was not laughing. She kept her face locked in a scowl. "You calling me a liar!?" she challenged the woman next to her, with a glare which she underlined by aggressively flinging a wet rag.

The laughter petered out, then Lily said slowly and clearly, "I swear he was 72 years old when he was born," before adding in a sincere tone, "Well that's what my dear old mammy told me, anyhow. And she also told me another thing." Again she paused to allow the drama to build. When the silence was sufficiently ripe, she rather loudly whispered as though entrusting us all with an important secret, "Actually, he's the Yellow Emperor in disguise. Yes, the Yellow Emperor himself! Over two thousand years old!" As a sort of admission she added, "But he wasn't living in our town the whole time."

The revelation was met by sniggers of laughter. Sue was happy to prod the game along. "So, Lily, is he really yellow?"

"Hell, I don't know!"

"What, you've never been up to call on the Yellow Emperor?"

"And what would I have to say to the Yellow Emperor!?" shouted Lily, laughing raucously as though that was the punch-line of her joke, and everyone else was allowed to laugh along.

'It's just one of those laughing days,' I thought to myself, disappointed not to have received any sort of answer to my question. I shook my head and carried on with the washing.

As I rinsed the clothes, the women's gossip lost my interest and I started listening to the table of lads sitting outside the inn. Their discussions had become part of my regular entertainment on washing mornings. They usually sat at the same table, back away from the road. I guessed that their presence there might have something to do with Kim, the inn-keeper's daughter. I had noticed that their eyes followed her each time she emerged carrying pots of tea or jugs of wine. Kim was scrubbing the unused tables and I wondered whether that was why they were speaking so loudly. One of them was describing his ideas of 'universal love'. He said that the world would be much better if everyone loved everybody else unconditionally. His friends didn't appear to be very interested in his lengthy arguments in favour of universal love. It seemed they had heard him speaking on that subject before.

The tall lad interrupted the dour monologue in an equally loud voice, "Oh Mo, universal love will never happen. Doing to others as you would have them do unto you is all that you can ever hope to achieve." Mo almost shouted his response, but I noticed that Kim wasn't paying much attention to the lads' discussion. She seemed more interested in the tables she was cleaning.

But then Sue whispered, "Look out," nodding her head in the direction of our lane. I was horrified to see that she was referring to Yan, who had just wandered into the square. Without the entertainment of my housework to hold his attention, it seems that he had taken it upon himself to explore the town.

"Oh no," I said, turning my face from his direction, hoping he wouldn't see me. I imagined him coming to stare at me while I did the washing, constantly asking his questions while all the women looked on. What would Lily and the others make of that?

There was a moment of relief when Yan strolled to the other side of the square and up to the gateway of the town hall. He went through, but soon came out again. My heart sank when he then started walking past the fountain and across the square towards the inn and the washing slabs.

I was keeping my head down, trying to finish the washing as fast as I could but ready to gather it up at any minute, rinsed or not. Then, just as I thought Yan had seen me, he stopped. He just stood there, staring into mid-air.

I hoped that none of the washers had noticed his strange behaviour. Luckily they were preoccupied, hooting and screaming at a bawdy story one of the women had related. It became apparent that Yan had stopped to listen to the lads' conversation. He walked over to their table and said simply, "Are you boys discussing benevolence and righteousness?"

I tried to melt into the washing, fearing that my lamb-like guest was due for an embarrassing slaughter at the hands of the local lads, with the washer-women probably joining in for the kill. I was wrong.

The question was met coldly but not aggressively. Mo said, "No, we're talking about universal love."

"Oh," said Yan, "is that in accord with the ways of the sage-kings of old?"

"Yes! Yes, it is," enthused Mo, suddenly warming to the stranger. "Why, do you study the kings of old?"

"Yes. I study with the greatest scholar of the age, the great Confucius. He is staying here in this town at this very moment."

I had finished the washing and was gathering it up, preparing to make a stealthy exit, but then I saw Yan's 'great master' walking into the square. "Here comes my master now!" announced Yan brightly. I decided to re-rinse a pair of trousers until Confucius had passed, otherwise I would have been forced to meet my colourful cousin in front of my washing colleagues.

As master and pupil greeted each other, I took the opportunity to slip away, whispering a quick cheerio to Sue who responded by nodding and squeezing up her face into a conspiratorial grin. Without looking back, I skirted around the square and made my way to the alleyway that leads to the short cut home.

It was a relief that I made it to our lane without being seen together with my visitors and it wasn't long until I saw Sue coming back with her washing. She shouted out to me cheerfully, "Quite some guests you've got there, again!"

I went next door to find out what had happened after I had left.

"Your cousin was giving that table of lads a lesson. That was all really. He certainly seems to know a lot, doesn't he," said Sue, smoothing the wrinkles from a pair of trousers.

"Oh," I said, relieved that nothing more embarrassing had occurred.

"Yes, they seemed quite keen. Except that lad, Ian. He said he was only interested in pretty girls, fine clothes, good food, and getting himself a large luxurious house with lots of servants. And that other lad as well, Mo, he was a bit put-out. Your cousin said his 'universal love' was unfilial or something."

"What?" I asked.

"I don't know. Apparently, if you love everyone as much as your family, it's disrespectful to your parents or something, which Mo did not like at all. They had a bit of a slanging match about old kings, but then Lily had to get involved, of course. She shouted out that if they want to know about old kings they should go and ask the yellow emperor, he lives up the hill there. Your cousin's face was a picture. For a moment I swear I thought he actually believed her! He looked like he'd seen a ghost."

It had been a couple of days since Confucius and Yan arrived. I had originally assumed they were stopping for just one night and I was getting a little concerned that they still hadn't mentioned leaving. I heard that Confucius had been spending time with some of the local lads and I was beginning to feel that Sue's joke about us running a school wasn't so funny after all. Just when I was beginning to think I should have a word with my cousin, he returned from the market with news. He had met a fellow scholar who told him about the ruler of a neighbouring province who was fond of learning and who might possibly grant him an audience. After hearing of this new prospect, Confucius's excitement had risen visibly. He had also bought some new divining sticks. A little later, I came into the house to find him casting the sticks and sorting them into piles. His new sticks seem to have told him what he wanted to hear. He was delighted with the prediction, and so was I. The sticks had revealed he should change his plans, to journey instead across the border to the next state.

The next day, we stood at the door as they prepared to depart. Yan held the mounting cord for his master. Confucius had a determined look. He stood erect for a moment before taking the cord and climbing up. As they drove off, he raised his hand to us without even turning his head. I silently wished the foreign king luck and wondered what he would make of my intense cousin. At least a palace could afford to put them up better than we could. I heard Confucius describe himself as a man for whom learning was such a passion that he even forgot to eat. Well I certainly hadn't noticed.

6. ANOTHER VISITOR!

It had been a slightly awkward shock when Cousin Confucius appeared at my door, but it was a wonderful surprise when I answered a knock on the door a few months later to find my cousin Leah standing there, with her husband and a baby. She proudly introduced her little girl, then I quietly took them into the house to show off my own sleeping baby boy. They had come for the autumn festival which was always the biggest celebration in the town's calendar. That year it was an especially big event as the king had left a prize of ten gold pieces for the archery competition.

The king had declared the prize when he had visited the town a few weeks earlier. The visit had not been planned. His carriage had lost a wheel in a badly rutted section of the road where it forks to meet the ferry. I heard that he wore a black expression as he walked into town trailing a band of nervous courtiers, and that he swore colourfully at the officials who had come running out of the town hall to meet him.

Fixing the wheel was only going to take a few minutes so, after casting a disdainful glance around the square, the king decided he would take some tea at the inn. Ignoring the inn-keeper's deep bow and welcoming indication of the open door, he sat himself down at one of the tables outside.

"Just tea!" he barked, in a manner which only a royal highness could get away with. He then took a book from a pocket in his gown. He continued to scowl while he started to read. The scowl only softened when Kim came to serve his tea. After Kim had gone he returned to his book and to his scowl.

It wasn't many minutes before the wheelwright approached the king's groom who was loitering at a safe but attentive distance from the foul-tempered king. The wheelwright and the groom exchanged words, then the groom walked up to the king and passed on the message. The king did not look happy.

"Come!" came the royal command, with the groom indicating to the wheelwright to hurry his approach.

The wheelwright explained to the king that the repair might take longer than expected as the bits of metal which fix the wheel to the axel had been shaken loose and were not with the carriage. Apparently they were of a size that he didn't stock so, unless the wheelwright's son could find them back along the road, it would mean either sending back to the capital for replacements or getting the metal-workers to make new ones, either of which would take a considerable time.

"Well in that case, let us hope that your lad can find them," said the king in an ominously calm voice, accompanied by the kind of stare which can cost people their lives, or their feet. He returned to his reading and the audience was clearly over. Perhaps it was the wheelwright's natural friendliness which prompted him, instead of sensibly retreating to safety, to enquire what the king was reading.

The king was visibly startled by the presumptuous question, coming as it did from someone who was clearly one of the commonest of commoners. "I am reading the authorities, the sages," he exclaimed haughtily.

"Oh," acknowledged the wheelwright, "and would those sages be alive or dead?"

"Dead, of course, dead for a long time," uttered the king, clearly resenting the intrusion.

"Well in that case, Your Majesty, all you're reading is the dirt they left behind," said the wheelwright as a simple matter of fact, in the same tone he would use when speaking to anyone.

"What!?" The king laughed, though it wasn't the sort of laugh to invite participation. It was the sort of laugh that stops anyone else laughing, and one which made the blood drain from the cheeks of those present. "How dare *you*, a mere wheelwright, comment on the reading of a king? You shall die for your impertinence," thundered the king, adding with a sinister laugh, "unless, of course, you can make good your assertion."

One of the guards ran up to apprehend the condemned man.

"No, we'll hear his explanation," said the king solemnly, adding quietly, "There's precious little else in this town to amuse us."

"Well, I can only explain it as a man of my craft," started the wheelwright, as though not understanding that he was arguing for his life. "When I make a wheel, I know that if I make it too softly, though that might be quite pleasant, it doesn't make for a good wheel. If, on the other hand, I hit it too hard I get too tired and the thing doesn't work anyway. So when making a wheel I have to hold it in my hand, and hold it in my heart, and feel the right way to hit it. It's not something I can really describe. Even if Your Majesty were to try to beat it out of me, I couldn't tell you how I do it. So even with my own lad, who I am trying to train-up for it, it's not something I can simply tell him, or something he can simply grasp. If I could write, and I wrote down a thousand words about it, it wouldn't help. That's why I still have to make all the wheels, though I live in hope that one day my son might acquire the knack. That is just my knowledge about making a wheel. It's the same with the ancient ones. When they died they took their knowledge with them. The words in the books, well that's nothing but the rubbish they left behind."

As the wheelwright finished his humble explanation the king had a little smile and was nodding his head. And then he laughed, but this time the royal laugh was one which did invite his subjects to join in. He threw his arm round the shoulder of the wheelwright and said, "You know, you're absolutely right. Not only that but, now you mention it, this is also quite the dullest book I have ever had the misfortune of trying to read!" With that he tossed the book into the road and it was smiles all round.

The happy scene was completed by the wheelwright's son who came running up clutching a bit of metal in each hand, shouting out in a fashion most unbefitting the royal presence, "I found them Dad!"

But now the king was in much better spirits. "Excellent!" he said. And then, noticing the boxes outside the town hall for entrants to the various competitions at the forthcoming festival, he announced in an official, kingly-sounding voice, "In honour of the brave lesson I have just received here, I have decided to provide a purse of ten gold coins to be awarded to the winner of the, er, archery competition."

Leah didn't say whether the king's golden prize was the real reason for their trip, but it was great to see her again. She told me they had come to the festival to help a merchant from their own town and that they were staying with the merchant's relatives. Many people journeyed to our town for the autumn festival. It was said that the town's population doubled at festival time.

That year's festival was the first time that Sue's husband, Dan, held a stall to raise funds for a communal ancestor shrine. For some reason he had decided that the few scattered houses along our lane should have their own shrine. It seemed a strange idea when we all had different ancestors, but his efforts certainly added to the sense of community in the neighbourhood. Chuey didn't seem to have any objections to the shrine, though neither did he show any enthusiasm for getting involved, so I had offered to help. I contributed rice-cakes and said I'd take a turn manning the stall.

As we set up the stall it was obvious that Dan was already getting agitated, which was unusual for this solidly-built man. I asked him if he was nervous about the afternoon's competition. He seemed offended. "Nervous!? No. Not at all." He added that he was looking forward to it, forcing a tight smile to reinforce his words, but his grimace only seemed to confirm quite the opposite. As soon as the stall was ready he hurried off to his bow and arrows for a spot of last minute practice.

After my shift on the stall, Leah came over. It was getting close to the time of the archery competition and I was already feeling nervous for the competitors. "I wonder how the men are feeling," I said as we jostled through the crowd to find a place with a good view, but everyone else was trying to do the same.

"Oh, don't worry about my husband," said Leah dismissively, "nerves won't affect him. He'll be fine."

I was surprised at Leah's confidence. I was fairly sure that Chuey wouldn't be nervous either, but there was a big difference. Leah's husband was competing for ten gold coins whereas Chuey was only competing for a pot of honey. I had tried to talk Chuey into entering the archery contest instead of fencing but he had laughed at the suggestion.

We weren't having any success in our struggle to find a vantage point. Luckily Joe saw us and he beckoned us over to a cart which was acting as part of the barrier to the competitors' enclosure. Carefully handing up the babies, we managed to climb onto the cart where we could sit comfortably with a fine view of the proceedings.

The competition was unusually long-winded due to the large number of entrants, but that only served to heighten my nerves further. Sue had excitedly listed all the things you could do with ten gold coins and I could hear her voice growing ever shriller as she cheered Dan through the early rounds. With each of his successes I had become more convinced that I did not want my neighbours to win the coins. I'd like to pretend that was because I was supporting Leah and her husband, but in truth my thoughts were more mean-spirited than that. I felt a little guilty each time I found myself hoping that Dan would miss and that his opponents would not. In spite of my wishes, it seemed that all of Dan's practice would pay off. He was emerging as the crowd's favourite as it became increasingly partisan in cheering for the locals. The support became totally one-sided when it became clear that the deciding round would be between Dan and Leah's husband.

As they moved the target further away for the final, I could feel my stomach tense up. Leah hardly seemed interested in the affair. "Aren't you nervous?" I asked her with amazement.

Leah was enjoying showing off her total faith in the outcome. "Nervous? What of? The prize is ours, I told you." Leah's confidence had some justification. Each time her husband had shot a set he had hardly seemed to take aim, barely pausing between arrows, yet they had all flown to the centre of the target as if by magic.

The two finalists bowed to each other. Dan had his features set in a look of grim determination, Leah's more slightly built husband still seemed perfectly at ease. The referee drew straws and indicated that Leah's husband was to go first. He raised his bow, pulling back the string and Thft, Thft, Thft, three bull's-eyes, which drew disappointed mumbles from the crowd.

Then it was Dan's turn. There were a few encouraging shouts until the referee held up his hand for silence. Dan raised his bow but then lowered it again and stared hard at the target. He raised this bow a second time, drew the arrow back and Thft. A bull's-eye, which was met with cheers from the crowd and I could hear Sue shrieking her encouragement. The referee held his hand up again.

Dan took his next arrow, rolled it between his fingers and thumb, then discarded it and took another. Thft, another bull's-eye and even louder cheers. Dan seemed to be growing in confidence. I could see the muscles in his cheek clenching his jaw as he focussed on the target for his third arrow. Thft.

A few half-cheers died away to a tense murmuring. Dan's third arrow seemed to be just on the edge of the centre-circle. The referee walked to inspect the target then announced in a loud voice, "Bull's-eye!" and the crowd gave a loud roar. Dan saluted them.

The target was moved back another couple of paces ready for the next set. Leah's husband stepped up, raised his bow and Thft, Thft, Thft. The arrows all struck the middle of the target. He hadn't even paused for the referee to silence the boos.

I heard Sue anxiously shout out to Dan that he could do it. Dan walked up to the mark. He fitted an arrow to his bow-string, but then decided to pace up and down for a while. He started to raise his bow but thought better of it and wiped his forehead with the back of his hand. He seemed to be swallowing hard and his large face seemed a little redder than it should have been. I could see him taking deep breaths and for a moment I feared he might be having a seizure. As I watched him struggle to breathe, my hopes made a strange reversal. I found that I was starting to feel for Dan in his big moment and, suddenly, I did not want him to miss.

He raised his bow, pulled back the string and held it, and continued to hold it – too long surely. When he finally let go, the arrow flew way off target, hitting the stand not much higher than the ground.

The crowd was silent. A few commiserating comments were shouted. Dan stood there like a broken man and I suddenly felt ashamed for having hoped he would lose. Leah was annoyingly unmoved by the victory, saying smugly, "See Cousin, what did I tell you."

I tried to show a similar level of faith that Chuey would win the fencing, but I couldn't stop myself asking Leah how she had been so sure that her husband would remain calm. She said that it was all down to his archery tutor. On his first lesson her husband had demonstrated his technique, successfully hitting the target, but the tutor, rather than congratulating him, asked him if he knew why he had hit the target. As he did not know, the tutor sent him away, telling him to come back when he had learned the purpose of archery.

"The purpose?" I asked, "Why?"

Leah just shrugged. She said it was three years before he went back, but apparently it had really helped. She said that now he could shoot straight even in an earth-quake, and that's how she knew he wouldn't be affected by nerves.

"Oh." I said, and hoped that Chuey wouldn't look too nervous when the fencing started.

By the time of the fencing competition, most of the crowd had already dispersed. Fewer people had entered than usual and, after the drama of the archery shoot-out, no one seemed very interested. The final proved to be something of a mismatch, with Chuey's opponent hardly able to mount an attack let alone score any hits. Chuey won easily and I smiled proudly as he collected the prize, even if it was only a pot of honey.

I was pleased with the day, though it didn't seem right that Leah's husband had received a pot of honey as well as the gold coins. That seemed unfair and it made me wonder whether Leah's husband had more of the Tao than Chuey. Still feeling guilty for my secret ill-wishes I took a cupful of the honey round to Sue and Dan's house.

At home that night I was quiet. Chuey asked if anything was wrong. I said, "It's just unlucky the king gave the prize for archery and not for fencing."

Chuey put a generous spoonful of honey on a rice-cake and said, "Maybe". He put his arm around me and offered me a bite.

"Maybe?" I queried. Chuey shrugged and took a bite. I laughed and repeated, "What? Maybe!?" Chuey simply shrugged again, as though he couldn't see that gold and honey was always going to be a whole lot better than just honey. I shook my head. Chuey again offered me a bite of the rice-cake. We were lucky enough I guess.

The following year both Chuey and Leah's husband won jars of honey again, but the year after that only one of them got to take home honey. The archery competition had started in its familiar fashion, with Leah's husband at his usual, predictable best. People had started to boo each time his three swift shots struck the centre of the target but, unlike the booing when there was gold at stake, this was good-natured, a sort of grudging compliment. The competition would have meandered to the same conclusion as the previous two years but for a mysterious stranger who had the same rapid-fire technique, with the same unerring accuracy. Dan had failed to progress, walking away shaking his head, leaving Leah's husband to face the stranger in the final.

The final turned into a marathon, the target having been moved back four times without a hint of either man failing to hit the centre. Never before had it taken five sets to decide the final and people were looking on in amazement, wondering what it would take to make either of them miss.

At that point the stranger said, "You shoot well, but that is merely mundane archery. It is not the non-archery of the true artist. What if we were to continue the competition up there?" He pointed to the rocky crags overlooking the town. Leah's husband seemed pleased to accept the stranger's strange challenge so, to the surprise of all present, the competition adjourned to the cliff top.

Dan told me later what had happened when they reached the top of the crags. The stranger had walked right to the edge, where the drop is highest and sheerest. He turned his back to the cliff and stepped back, until he was standing with his heels jutting out into thin air, balancing only on the front part of his feet. After bouncing up and down on his toes for a moment he raised his bow, and pulled back the arrow, ready to shoot. He then called for Leah's husband to join him.

Leah's husband walked to the edge and looked over. He too turned his back to the cliff and shuffled his feet back slightly, carefully looking down to see how close he was to the drop. With another little shuffle, and another, his heels were just level with the edge, but sweat was breaking-out on his forehead and his hands were shaking as he reached for an arrow and fumbled it into place. He tried, gingerly, to lift his bow. He began to draw back the string, his hands now shaking uncontrollably. He glanced down, past the quivering bow, to the great drop beneath him and for a moment froze. Suddenly casting his bow away, he lunged forward, gratefully grabbing at two tufts of grass. There he stayed for a moment, shaken by his self-imposed ordeal of vertigo. The stranger stepped forward, away from the cliff's edge, and the two men shared a smile, with Leah's husband giving a nod of respect, signalling his acceptance of the outcome of the competition.

I wondered what Leah would have made of her husband's cliff-top antics. I certainly wouldn't have been pleased if Chuey had behaved in such an irresponsible way, not with a wife and young family to support. And all for a pot of honey! I allowed myself a gentle dig, suggesting that perhaps her husband hadn't entirely conquered his nerves after all. Ignoring my comment, she merely said, "Boys will be boys."

Chuey had seen the start of the archery competition but hadn't heard about the happenings at the top of the cliff as he had been busy winning his own competition. When I told him what Dan had described of the adventure he just gave a little laugh, which reminded me of the first time I had seen him, after Confucius had made his hasty exit from the funeral. Chuey was still very much a man of mystery. And he was also bearing a big pot of honey again which was something, on that day, Leah could not say of her husband.

One of the nice things to come out of Leah's trips to the autumn festival is that I became friendly with the merchant in town who Leah stayed with. I often saw her at the market, particularly after she started to take my spinning. She would supply bags of ramie fluff and was happy to take as much yarn as I could spin. As the merchant regularly traded with her relative, the merchant who Leah had come to the festival with, it was a nice bonus that I got to enjoy occasional updates on Leah and her family.

He who knows (the Tao) does not (care to) speak (about it); he who is (ever ready to) speak about it does not know it.

TAO TE CHING CHAPTER 56

7. USELESS

I don't know what happened then, but it all started to change. I don't think Chuey changed, I don't think he's ever changed, so I suppose it was me. I started to find Chuey's visitors and all of the endless philosophising annoying. I came to agree with Cousin Confucius. I once heard him say, "There's something hopeless about a group of men sitting talking all day without hitting upon a single truth, wanting only to show off their cleverness." That certainly seemed to describe Chuey's discussions with his visitors. And there seemed to be more and more of them. We didn't see the duke again but his younger companion returned a few times. On one of his visits I remember him saying that he had come to hear more about the Tao. Instead, Chuey started talking about another of his favourite subjects, 'nothingness'. I heard him telling the visitor one of his stories. He said that Star-light asked Non-being, "Master, do you exist or do you not exist?" Apparently Star-light was then very impressed at not receiving an answer. "Perfect!" said Star-light "The furthest point yet! I can comprehend the absence of being, but who can comprehend the absence of nothing? If, on top of that, Non-being exists, who can comprehend that?"

Well, I certainly couldn't comprehend it, though I could clearly comprehend the link between the lack of food in the house and the constant stream of visitors. How could discussing 'the absence of nothing' or the 'existence of Non-being' be in any way helpful? The young gentleman didn't seem to share my views. He had a strange smile on his face and was nodding as though off in some ecstatic trance. When he left, he thanked Chuey warmly.

After our third child was born, our tiny house simply wasn't big enough to accommodate the toddlers, babies and philosophers. Hearing Chuey yet again telling some stranger that an ideal man doesn't feel emotion, I remember feeling quite a lot of emotion as I tried to manage the children in our cramped, invaded space.

There were other real concerns. Our livelihood depended on the fish Chuey caught. When it had just been Chuey and I, grazing on wild plants in nature's larder had been an adventure. That lost its appeal when our growing children were going hungry. I felt angry when we had little or nothing to sell on market day. Chuey always had a ready excuse. Either the frost would have stopped the fish biting, or the water would be too coloured after rain, but I blamed the visitors and all the philosophising. I blamed the Tao!

My hazy frustrations grew over time, then a visit from Leah helped them take on a more certain shape. Leah had not come to the festival the previous year so I was pleased to learn from the merchant she would be coming that year. When she arrived I was surprised that her husband was not with her. At first Leah just said that he was busy at home. I only learned the full story when she came round to our house. She brought just the baby, leaving her other youngsters playing with the merchant's children. After we had settled down with a cup of tea she started to tell me the real reason her husband had stayed at home.

Leah described how her husband had been studying under some sort of teacher when he had heard about a shaman who lived in a nearby town. Apparently the shaman could accurately tell a person the date they had been born and exactly predict the day they would die. Leah's husband went to see the shaman and concluded that this man knew more than his teacher. The teacher heard of this and instructed Leah's husband to bring the shaman to him.

After they had met, the shaman took Leah's husband aside and told him that his teacher was gravely ill and only had a week to live. When told of this, the teacher told Leah's husband to bring the shaman to see him again. After his second visit the shaman reported that the teacher was now miraculously cured and would live a full life. The teacher then explained to Leah's husband that he was choosing how he appeared to the shaman. He asked to see the shaman a third time. Again the shaman came but soon ran out of the house in a crazed fear of the teacher. The teacher explained that this time he had made himself appear as 'hitherto unrevealed potential'. He had presented himself as 'not knowing who is who, nor what is what'. He said "I appeared flowing and changing as I wanted. That is why he bolted."

All of this had a strange effect on Leah's husband. After witnessing his teacher's dominance over the shaman, he gave up all of his pursuits and even stopped his studies. Instead he stayed at home, cleaning and cooking for Leah and the children. Leah said he also took rather good care of the pigs, waiting on them as though they were human. I later heard that it was three years before he would even leave the house.

We both sat in silence after Leah had finished her account. Then Leah said, shaking her head, "Oh Cousin, what have we done, marrying such men?"

It was disturbing to hear Leah mentioning Chuey in the same breath as her pig-waiter of a husband. I felt like pointing out the difference but, in my heart, I could see what she meant and I could feel something of her despair.

Another moment that helped to firm up my frustrations occurred one night when Hue visited. It was one of those long, warm summer evenings. Again I was spinning while the two men debated and, as usual, Hue's attack faltered, dashed on the immovable rocks of Chuey's 'pivot of the Tao'. This time Hue seemed particularly frustrated. He leaned back with resignation, sighed, folded his arms and sat there for a moment shaking his head. "I don't know," he said. "Your words are big, but they lack any practical application. They remind me of some gigantic gourds I grew a while ago. They were the largest, most impressive gourds anyone had ever seen, but when I came to decide what to do with them I was stumped. I tried using them to hold water, but when they were filled they were too heavy to carry. I cut them in half to make scoops, but they were so large that the scoops were awkward to use. So even though the gourds had looked impressive there was no practical application of them. We ended up throwing them on the fire."

Chuey started to speak, but Hue was suddenly excited about the new line of attack he had stumbled upon. "No, admit it, it's useless! What you say is all totally useless! It is like that great big tree on my land. It might be big, but no carpenter would ever look at it. Its trunk is knotted and its branches are all twisted. You couldn't get a single straight, useful bit of timber out of the whole tree." Hue was enjoying his advantage. "Your words are as useless as that tree! And that is why, I am afraid to say, everyone ignores them! I mean, look at you. Do you try to be useless!?"

"No," laughed Chuey "I once heard about a farmer who had two cockerels. One crowed and the other didn't. When it was time to eat one of them he decided to eat the one that was less useful. That's why I try to stay somewhere between useful and useless."

Hue waved away Chuey's light-hearted response. He was still sitting smugly with his arms folded and seemed convinced that he had done enough.

After a pause, Chuey said in a more measured tone, "My dear friend, have you considered that the problem might lie with yourself and not with my words? From what you say, it seems to me that you are unable to use big things. Couldn't you have used your great gourds to make floats to help you float down rivers and lakes? And your tree, can you not fall asleep in its shade? What is there in its 'uselessness' to cause you distress? Everyone knows the usefulness of the useful, but few indeed know the usefulness of the useless."

Hue returned to shaking his head with a weary frustration at the game. He might not have agreed with the 'sense' of Chuey's response, but he could see that his efforts to tie Chuey down to a submission were futile. Chuey had once more side-stepped the attack, dancing around Hue's accusation of uselessness by refusing to accept his uselessness as a bad thing.

Hue's claim that Chuey's ideas were useless stuck in my mind, and that thought was echoed a day or two later. I was doing my washing and, as usual, I was listening to the conversation of the lads sat at the table outside the inn. They started discussing their intended careers. The two lads called Mensa and Hussain wanted to enter government. I was amazed to hear Mensa mention that he wanted to be 'something like Confucius'. Mo also seemed to think his destiny lay with teaching the rulers how to rule. Ian didn't seem to mind what he did as long as it afforded him luxury and pretty women. Only the lad called Hans seemed to have any practical thoughts. He eventually managed to say that he was hoping to study law. I had heard Hans struggling with a bad stutter, at times unable to get his words out at all, but even with his speech impediment Hans's plan sounded a lot more practical than those I had just heard from his friends.

The lads' ambitions might have been farfetched but at least they had some ambition. Their discussion set me thinking about Chuey and his profession, or lack of profession. I could see that this all went together with Hue's comment that Chuey's words and ideas were useless. With three children already, and another one on the way, it was a worrying thought.

That time marked the first stirrings of a worry which went much deeper than any reservations I might have had about his philosophising. It was the start of a kind of unspoken tug-of-war between us. Well, from me to Chuey at least. I cannot say I ever noticed him pulling or pushing back, or reacting to any of my hints and comments.

It is strange, the patterns which fate throws up. It was while I was eavesdropping on the lads' career plans, and comparing them with Chuey's uselessness and lack of ambition, that Sue decided to use a lull in the conversation to make her big announcement to the fifth-day washing regulars. She told us that she and Dan would soon be moving to a new house on the other side of town. "Very posh!" said one of the women when Sue described the location.

"And even though I'm going to be a fine lady from now on, I'll still come and wash with you scrubbers!" she joked.

There was a general good-natured response to Sue's light-hearted insult, but I was still lost in my thoughts. How could Dan and Sue afford that? I had always thought them to be as poor as Chuey and I. My first thoughts were about the funds for the new ancestor shrine, which had still not been built. I swallowed the negative thoughts and told Sue I was very happy for her. She said she would be sad to leave our little neighbourhood, but her excited smile as she talked about the details of her new house suggested she wasn't really too grieved to be leaving us.

Dan had not been dipping into the Ancestor Shrine fund. The only connection was that the money was coming from Dan's arrow making, which he had originally started as a way to raise funds for the shrine. Since then it had grown into a profitable side-line, so much so that it had grown to become his full time business. From selling small numbers of arrows to a few interested amateurs, he had entered into a contract with the local metal works, increased his production, and had obtained a regular order from the army. All of this was a great surprise to me. Sue explained that they had felt the need to keep it quiet, adding, "Well, you know what people round here are like." If I hadn't known before, I was certainly learning.

I was sad to lose Sue as a neighbour. She had been my friend, my mid-wife and child-minder, but she stayed true to her word and kept her spot next to me on wash-day mornings, with the rest of us 'scrubbers', for a while at least.

8. EARNING

I never expected Chuey's fishing to make us rich but as the children grew it seemed more and more obvious that he had little interest in adequately providing for us. Instead of working hard to support his growing family, he seemed more interested in his philosophising. One event showed Chuey's strange priorities in a way that would leave just about anyone sympathising with my frustration.

Chuey had left in the morning for a day's fishing. When he came back he told me that he had been offered a job but that he had turned it down. "Oh," I said, surprised that anyone would offer Chuey a job, assuming it to have been some seasonal casual work. "What sort of job?"

"Er, working as, er, an official," he said rather sheepishly. At first I thought he was joking, but he assured me he was not. I was speechless. I had seen the town officials getting fatter as we had found it ever harder to make our humble ends meet. I asked what the pay would have been. He said that it had not been discussed. "You mean you turned it down without even asking about the money!?" I was very upset and ran out of the house to hide my angry tears.

The next day I set off with my washing, as usual on the fifth day. I thought people had been looking at me strangely as I carried my washing to the slabs. I felt my hair and checked my clothes but no, there was nothing obviously wrong. Then, when I arrived at the slabs, all of the other women were already there, with a few extras just standing around. That was unusual. My usual slab, next to Sue, was free. I heard one of them say, "Ooh, here she is!" Apart from that, no one was talking. Again, unusual.

"What? What's wrong?" I asked, cautiously.

Sue said, "Well, is it true?"

I wondered what she meant, but then I remembered Chuey's news. "What, you mean the job offer?" I ventured.

"The job offer!!!" they all screamed, as though I had just told the funniest joke anyone had ever heard.

Sue stared at me, in wide-eyed amazement. "So it is true! I assumed it was just a joke."

"No," I said warily, sensing that there was something wrong with the level of interest being shown in Chuey's refusal of some work.

Sue stared at me with her mouth wide open. "Oh, you poor love. Well, what did you think?"

"Well I was annoyed," I said honestly, which was met with a peel of yet more raucous laughter from the women.

"She was annoyed! Could have been the prime minister's wife and she was *annoyed*!" shouted one of the women while they all rolled around, helpless with laughing.

I was dazed. Sue looked at me compassionately and said, "Oh, pet." I looked back at her, and I looked at the other women collapsed in their hysterics. I was just dazed.

From my 'friends' at the washing-slabs, and from many other conversations over the next few days, I came to realise that the work Chuey had turned down had not been merely the comfortable job in the town hall that I had imagined. When I challenged him on his sparing use of the truth, Chuey told me the whole story, though to be honest, there wasn't really much else to tell.

Apparently he had been fishing when two senior court officials approached him with a message from the king saying, "Might I trouble you to administer my lands?"

Chuey replied that he had heard that the king kept an ancient sacred turtle shell in his ancestral temple, carefully wrapped in silk. "Do you think the turtle would have wanted to have died and to have been so venerated, or do you think that it would have preferred to have carried on living a natural life, dragging its tail round in the mud?" The officials had to give the obvious answer that the turtle would have preferred to have lived. Then, without looking up from his fishing float, Chuey had told them, "Well shove off then. And I'll carry on dragging my tail around in the mud."

And that was the whole story. Instead of 'rags to riches' I had to suffer 'rags to rags with ridicule'. "You watch your language in front of the prime minister's wife!" they would say. "Oh no, I remember now, Chuey turned down the *job offer*!" It was a long time before I could smile along.

Aside from the joking, there was a subtle change in people's attitude. I might not have been a courtier, but I could have been. And even if Chuey was one of the poorest men in the town, at least everyone knew that there was some choice in our situation. I came to value that crumb of respect.

Even with everyone else's apparent acceptance of the fact that Chuey had been offered, and had turned down, the post of prime minister, it hardly felt real to me until a visitor arrived a few days later. It was one of the occasional regulars, the same well-dressed young gentleman I had first seen in the company of the duke.

Chuey welcomed him warmly and said he had suspected that the visitor had been behind all of this. The gentleman admitted that yes, he might have influenced the interpretation of oracle a little. They both chuckled at that. The gentleman said that he should have realised that Chuey wouldn't be interested in being prime minister and begged his forgiveness for troubling him with the offer. Chuey waved the apology away as though it were nothing, perhaps not realising the level of teasing I was having to endure.

As the one-time duke's companion was leaving, he turned back and quoted, "Dragging your tail around in the mud." Pointing at Chuey, he shook his head laughing, as though being tickled. Repeating "in the mud", he glanced around our little house somewhat wistfully, even enviously I thought. Then he laughed again and was still shaking his head and laughing as he left.

As the gentleman's fine carriage drove away, Chuey leaned his head towards me and said quietly, "Sorry, I should have introduced you. That was, er, the prince."

I thought back to the charred brittle-cakes I had presented to him when I first saw him with the duke, and back to all my surly tea serving on his previous visits. The thought made me feel queasy with nerves. Perhaps it was a good thing that I wasn't going to be the prime minister's wife.

Chuey knew I was disappointed and explained something of his reasoning about the 'job offer' episode. He said it was a position which often costs the life of anyone who holds it, and one which always costs their peace of mind. I could see that there was some truth in his words, but what helped more was the memory of the prince, the king's son and heir, looking at our home and our lives with envy. For some reason, that image helped me to bear my lot.

Our new status as 'not-the-prime-minister' and 'not-the-prime-minister's-wife' might have eased my pride but it did nothing to ease any pangs of hunger. The situation eased a little when Chuey started making sandals. Chuey had first made them for the children, then he had made a pair for himself and then for a few of his friends. They were ingenious, held on with a strap that simply fastened by folding back on itself. The novel design was popular, but I think Chuey was embarrassed to be seen selling them. Instead he let one of the market-traders do that for us. Chuey never made much money from the sandals. As with the fish, he gave away as many as he sold.

Our situation further improved when I started to earn some money myself. Chuey had introduced me to the potter shortly after I arrived in town. The pottery was just around the hill from our house, up a track that led off the lane just before the bridge. When we had arrived it seemed as though the potter had been expecting us. After a polite enquiry as to how I was finding life in the town the potter said, "Right, let me show you around." Chuey and I followed him across the yard, past stacks of various pottery items, to his workshop.

The potter proceeded to describe the process of producing pots, first telling us about the clay he used and how he prepared it. Then he pointed at the contraption in the middle of the floor saying, "And this is the wheel." It looked like one of the great stone disks that millers use to grind grain, but it had a solid wooden frame around it. A plank of wood attached to the frame served as a seat.

The potter sat on the seat and started describing the process of fashioning a pot. While he spoke, his foot casually pushed the stone which turned slowly, and continued to turn. The potter continued his explanation but I just stared at the slowly turning wheel and interrupted him. "How does it keep turning?"

The potter gave a little smile, delighted that I had noticed. "That is our family's little secret. This wheel was built by my great-grandfather. My father showed me the secret and one day, if he is interested, I will pass it on to my son."

The potter pointed to the short log which was attached, upright, to the centre of the slowly turning stone. "And this is my contribution." He patted the flat top of the log, which rotated slowly with the wheel but which was otherwise perfectly still. "This raised turntable means I can sit up here, allowing me to work the wheel with my foot at the same time as making the pot. My father needed an assistant to push the wheel for him, but with this arrangement I can control the speed myself which is a great help. It also means I can work by myself which can be nice." The potter was clearly very proud of this innovation to his family's means of earning a living, though I remember thinking that sticking a log endways onto the centre of the wheel didn't seem that impressive.

He was describing how the clay is formed into shapes when the presentation took an unexpected practical turn. He put on an apron, pulled off a lump of clay and, after kneading it for a while, slapped it onto the top of the wooden column.

"The first thing is to centre the clay, so first we need to get some speed up." He wetted the clay with water from a bowl on the bench behind the wheel. He spoke purposefully, as though he thought we should be memorising the steps. While he talked us through the process, his leg kept pushing the great disc of stone which turned faster and faster until water was being flung off the turntable. The potter talked us through each of his actions, as an elegant looking pot took shape.

When the pot was finished Chuey and I were suitably impressed. The potter used his foot to gradually reduce the speed until he had brought the great stone disk to rest. Using a thin piece of twine he cut through the base of the newly formed pot which he then gently lifted from the wooden turntable and placed on the floor alongside other similar pots.

It had been an entertaining display, but then I was shaken out of my comfortable role of spectator when he said, "Right, do you want to have a go?" It was phrased as a question but the answer had already been assumed. The potter stood up, reached for one of the clean aprons hanging on the wall, and started putting the strap of the apron over my head before I had a chance to reply.

He slapped a lump of clay onto the flat top of the log in front of me and began, "Remember, first you have to centre the clay on the wheel." He repeated the instructions which had accompanied his own skilful movements a few moments earlier, but now it was me who was faced with a lump of clay revolving slowly on the turntable.

I tried to kick movement into the disk of stone. "No, much more speed," he demanded. I frantically tried to push with my foot without achieving any noticeable effect, the heavy stone remaining resistant to my struggles. Timing the pushes of my feet seemed impossible while wrestling awkwardly with the messy lump of wet clay which writhed in my hands in a very non-centred way.

The potter, realising that he had been expecting too much, then offered to work up the speed for me. My relief at his offer was short lived. After a small number of pushes, his leg had transformed the wheel into a whirl of motion, with an audible 'whiz'.

"Yes, not too fast. We'll keep it at this speed for the moment. It helps when centring the clay," he explained. But it didn't seem to help at all, the clay juddering uncontrollably in my hands. "Yes, that's right, now use the motion. Yes, yes just centre it," he instructed, not seeming to realise that was exactly what I was trying to do. I was struggling with all my might, as hard as I could, but the clay was not playing the game. It seemed to have a mind of its own. The more I tried to force it into the centre the more it violently kicked and jumped in my hands.

"Yes," said the potter slowly, not quite sure how to help me. "Yes, try locking your elbows against your body," he offered. I did as instructed but then my whole body was jerking with the effort and the clay's rebellious nature. I asked him if the violent jerks might break the log off the stone, but he assured me I could never budge that. Only partially reassured I struggled on, but the harder I tried the more the lump rebelled and my hands began to get thick with slime from the dissolving clay.

"Yes, I think you're getting there," he said charitably. "I'll just …, You don't mind, Chuey, do you?" Then he put his hands over mine and with a slight pressure magically caused the clay's violent spasms to dissolve. He took his hands away and all that was left between my palms was a perfect revolving stillness. For some reason the feeling sent a shudder down my spine.

"Right, so now we form the lump into the cake," he carried on, apparently indifferent to the miracle he had just performed. "Yes, and remember to keep it nice and wet. No, not too wet."

Then, with constant tips from the potter, I looked on with fascination as a pot took shape, growing almost effortlessly.

"Well, you've certainly got the knack," said the potter once a nice pot was spinning in front of me. I was amazed and very happy with the new creation. But then I thought that the neck ought to be a little narrower. I gave a slight inward push to the lip, and disaster struck! Within a spin of the wheel my lovely pot was reduced to a twisted pile of waste clay. Chuey and the potter laughed. I laughed as well, even though it was horribly disappointing.

After that first visit, the potter had invited me back to the pottery whenever we had chanced to meet. Then one day, I was crossing the square, walking home with the washing, when I literally bumped into him. Luckily I didn't drop the load, but the potter was mortified when he noticed that my clean damp washing now had clay-dust on it from his clothes. Neither of us had been looking where we were going and I was just as much to blame as he had been, but he was very apologetic. After a pleasant exchange the potter repeated his offer, saying that if I wanted to have another go on the wheel I would be welcome as some days it was unused. Previously I had made excuses, but that time I had good reasons for accepting. The number of mouths needing bowls had increased and the number of bowls had decreased, in the way they usually do, so I said 'yes please'.

It was with some tangible aims that I approached the pottery. Sadly, my needs didn't make much difference to my potting ability. The wish-list of items disappeared immediately I sat down at the wheel, and the session proved to be an almost complete rerun of that first lesson, all those years before. Eventually, with the potter's help, I produced two small bowls. He said he would be firing them soon and that they would be ready in a few days.

As I left, the potter asked if I would be coming back next week. I said no. He insisted that it's a very different game once you learn to centre the clay. I don't know why, but something in the way he spoke cut through my reluctance to accept yet more of his charity and I said 'yes, I would give it another go'. He seemed genuinely pleased, which made me doubly so.

After that, I started going to the pottery every week. The potter had been right. Once I acquired the knack of centring the clay it was a different game. I learned to impose my will on the rebellious clay with an intention which comes from deep down in the spine. I grew to love that change, when the violent jerks of the untamed clay clear to the mysterious stillness from which pots grow. As I became more accomplished, that stillness became my playground. I delighted in exploring the shapes which emerge from the peaceful centre of the wheel, from tall slender vases to low bulbous jars. I came to understand the potter's love of his craft.

Once I had satisfied my own pottery needs I started to make pieces for the potter. Money hadn't been mentioned, but we evolved a system of payment.

With the money from Chuey's fishing and sandal making, and my money from the potting and the pennies from the spinning, we usually had enough to get by. I never got to know what the prime minister's salary would have been, though I often used to think about it.

9. A SHRINE, EVENTUALLY

My weekly trip to the pottery helped me to stay sane, even through those chaotic years with a young family, and helped me cope with my frustration at a husband who was more interested in discussing nothingness than putting food in his family's bowls. Another thing that helped my state of mind was when we finally got our ancestor shrine built. Each year our stall at the festival had raised money for the shrine, but each time we achieved the goal Dan would come up with some new feature that he had seen in another neighbourhood's shrine and the target would be increased again. After Sue and Dan moved from the lane I assumed that the shrine would never be built, but as I had never really seen the need for a communal shrine I was happy to let the idea go.

It was a big surprise when Dan drove up one day, a few months after they had moved, and knocked on the door. He told me that he had engaged a builder and that construction of the shrine would be starting that week. He asked if I could keep an eye on things as he was rather busy, reassuring me that he'd pop in now and then.

The next day two geomancers arrived. One of them was short and well-built and the other one was taller and skinny. They were odd looking men and both of them seemed to be full of fun as they set about their task. The shorter one had a bendy stick, like a short version of one of Chuey's fishing rods but with a weight on the end. He bounced this weight up and down as he strode around with a gleeful look of fascination on his face and with his body almost bouncing in time. Every now and then he'd give a funny little hop as though he had been surprised by a snake. The taller one had a short metal rod with a bend in the middle. He would whirl the rod around above his head then follow whatever direction the rod pointed. As he walked, he stared hard at the tip of the rod, except when the effort got to be too much. Then he would stop to wipe his brow before shaking his head, whirling the rod around and setting off again.

Dan had already told me vaguely where he wanted the shrine to be built so I was surprised to see the geomancers walking way up the valley with their strange tools. The next time I looked, they had moved right down to the other side of the valley near the crown lands, where no one is supposed to go except the game-keepers. I laughed to myself, quite sure that wasn't where Dan would want the shrine to be built.

By lunchtime the geomancers seemed to be focusing on a patch of ground a little way up the valley from our house. They still seemed to be enjoying their work. After a while I heard some banging and went out to see them knocking a stake into the ground. I smiled as I watched, wondering what Dan would make of their positioning of the shrine. It looked as though the shrine would be built out in the gravel of the stream bed.

It was late afternoon before Dan drove up in his carriage. He walked over to the geomancers shaking his head vigorously and I heard him shouting "No!" as he pulled out the closest of the carefully positioned stakes. He walked twenty paces onto firmer ground and dropped the stake down, indicating with this arms where the walls should go. He seemed rather annoyed as he walked back to his carriage, quickly climbed up and drove away.

Once Dan had gone I saw the geomancers laughing as one of them retrieved the stake. After more careful checking with their tools, they placed it back in exactly the same hole that Dan had pulled it from. I couldn't help laughing too as I imagined what Dan's reaction might be.

The next day six men arrived on two wagons loaded with materials to begin the construction. I smiled each time I saw them placing the posts for the shrine on the positions marked by the geomancers. I was also quite shocked by the size. Rather than the little roadside shrine I had imagined, it was more like a small temple. I knew Dan's plans had grown rather grand, but I had not imagined a structure like that.

So we eventually had our communal ancestor shrine, even if most of the people involved in raising the funds had moved away from our lane by then. I had never been very interested in the shrine myself but two things changed that. The first was when I received news from Leah that both of my grandparents had died. Leah had stopped coming to the autumn festival, apparently because she was too busy. I had asked her merchant-friend what she was busy doing. She said that she didn't know but that "there are always a lot of shoes outside their house", so it sounded as though Leah's husband had even more visitors than Chuey. I wondered what Leah would think of that, and thought that perhaps I should start asking our visitors to remove their shoes before they came in.

Leah had asked the merchant to pass on the message about my grandparents' passing as she knew how close to them I had been. It shouldn't have been a surprise that my grandparents had died as they had already been quite old when I left, but the news had a big impact on me. I loved my grandparents. Apparently my grandmother had died first, quite peacefully, then my grandfather died within a month. That seemed fitting as I couldn't imagine what he would do without my grandmother to look after. I had been gone from my village for a long time, but I had never really thought it would have changed. Hearing that my grandparents were both dead made me think of all the other changes I was missing. How old would my parents be by then? I pictured them becoming elderly and eventually dying.

The other thing that gave me more interest in the new ancestor shrine was one of Cousin Confucius's visits. There had been a dramatic start to that visit. When Confucius had arrived, with Yan as usual, he was in a state of shock. His eyes were glazed, his face was the colour of ashes and he seemed barely able to breathe let alone speak. Eventually Yan was able to tell us that they had just returned from Robber Chih's camp. Robber Chih was the leader of a blood–thirsty gang of thieves, notorious for their brutality. We were amazed that Confucius and Yan had escaped unscathed.

Gradually my concerned questioning extracted the details from Yan. It turned out that Confucius had chosen to go to Robber Chih's camp voluntarily. Apparently the whole misadventure had started as a result of Confucius criticising Robber Chih's elder brother for not exercising more control over his wayward younger brother. It became clear that the real reason Confucius had gone to the camp of the notorious outlaw was to teach the robber's brother a lesson in brotherly duty. Confucius groaned at Yan's revelations, as though the memories were painful to him, but Yan continued. It seemed that Confucius had thought that he would be able to educate Robber Chih in the ways of the ancient kings, to teach him to be benevolent and righteous. As the details of the story emerged, my concern turned until, by the end,

I could have hit my cousin for risking his life, and Yan's life, on such a foolish mission.

Yan nervously delivered his account of what had occurred when Confucius had been granted an audience with the notorious thief. "My master told Robber Chih that he was a handsome, tall man who had lofty righteousness and that he was brave and eloquent."

"Oh, Robber Chih must have loved that," laughed Chuey.

"No," said Yan, shaking his head, still unable to comprehend how his master's plan had failed. "No, that made him even angrier. He thought the master was trying to win him over by flattery and promise of profit." Yan paused, frowned, shook his head and continued, "And he said the master was a driveller who merely credits his own rubbish to King Wen and Emperor Wu. He said that he eats without doing anything for his food, and that he preaches family relationships while always hoping to be given a place at court ahead of the king's relatives. He said the master should be called Robber Confucius." Chuey and I exchanged looks. But Yan had not finished telling tales.

"He said that the master cannot even take care of himself, yet he tries to tell the rest of the world how to live. He said that the master merely pronounces whatever he considers right and wrong and pretends his opinions have come from the ancient sage-kings to make them sound better. And he said that the master's way is foolish, deceitful, artful, vain and hypocritical."

At the end of Yan's account of Robber Chih's verbal abuse of my cousin, we all stood in silence, until Confucius said shakily that he would take a walk. After he had gone, Yan said, "Do you think the master will be alright?"

"Yes, perhaps you had better go and see," I suggested in a motherly tone, glad to see the back of them both, for the moment at least.

The next day Chuey was making himself scarce, as he often did when Confucius was staying. Yan had gone into town to see if he could find any of the local lads. Confucius seemed a little morose but generally recovered from his speechless state of the previous night. I admired his ability to constantly bounce back from his trials. I was still feeling rather angry towards him for putting himself and Yan in such a perilous situation so I decided to go outside to mend the fishing nets.

As I was walking past the open door with an armful of nets, I saw Confucius at our rather neglected little home ancestor shrine which occupied the end of a dusty shelf. I paused to see what he was doing. He was putting a bowl of fresh water on the shelf, after which he made a small bow.

I stood and watched my cousin honouring our ancestors. Confucius loved ritual, I knew that, but this was no empty ceremony. There was none of his acting or posturing. This was a simple, natural act and it was quite beautiful. Confucius noticed me watching. He wasn't at all self-conscious. He smiled. I smiled back and remembered why I have always been so fond of my earnest cousin.

After seeing Confucius's simple, honest ceremony honouring our ancestors, I took more of an interest in our lane's big, new shrine and would visit for a few moments every day. Each time I would silently thank the geomancers for picking that particular location for the shrine. I don't know whether some places are really any more special than others, but in the shrine I could believe it. The setting was spectacular, being at the very heart of the valley, but there also seemed to be a peace about the place. Walking into the shrine, you could feel it. It could almost take your breath away, in a very quiet sort of way. If there was anywhere that could help connect with the ancestors, that was the place. I also thanked Dan's ambitious plans. Having an enclosed space with a roof and a door made for a wonderful refuge from the elements and from whatever else I needed to retreat from.

My routine in the shrine was simple. I conducted a short ceremony, refreshing the cups and bowing, then I took a moment to think about my grandparents, and about their parents, who I never met, then about my grandparents' grandparents and those that went before them. I thought about my parents and me, and about my children. I would kneel, meditating on the whole chain of life.

Running forward, the thread comes to an end for each of us. Running backwards, the chain stretches on forever, through every generation, back to the start of life itself. And I thought about the fact that the same is true for all living things, each bug and each blade of grass. And I thought of how all of those threads interact. It isn't just ancestors that feed into us, but everything.

It was after such a meditation, as I was coming out of the ancestor shrine, that I looked up the valley and had the idea of taking some buns up to the old man who Confucius visited. Each time I had seen Confucius climbing the path to visit Lily's 'Yellow Emperor' I had wondered about him, though I had never considered walking up to introduce myself. Chuey had the children busy, helping with his sandal-making at the back of the house, and it was a nice day so I thought that visiting the old man would make for a nice walk. When I mentioned my plan Chuey laughed, but he thought it was a good idea and gave me rough directions.

I must admit that on that first visit I was motivated more by curiosity than by charity. The few times I had heard him mentioned hadn't given me much of an idea what to expect. Confucius had mentioned some of his comments, and I had heard Chuey quote him a few times. I hadn't taken Lily seriously, obviously, but her tales of him spending 72 years in his mother's womb had certainly added to my interest.

I followed the lane up the valley to where it narrowed to what looked like an animal track, past where the valley bent away to the right. Then I followed the track as it climbed away from the stream before turning left, up towards a notch at the top of the ridge. I was breathing hard by the time I rounded the edge of the crags. The walking became easier after that as the track levelled off and skirted the hill, then there, nestled in a small valley, stood the old man's house.

I walked up to the house but there was no sign that anyone was home. I knocked on the door. No answer. The door didn't seem to be latched so I pushed it open. I gave a sudden gasp. There sat the old man. He was sitting bolt upright, not moving at all, and he did have long ears just as Lily had said. He didn't seem to notice my arrival but kept looking straight ahead. "Er, hello," I ventured.

With my curiosity satisfied, I suddenly felt very self-conscious. "Well hello, I'm Chuey's wife," then I added with a little laugh, "your next-door-neighbour," which must have sounded as false as it felt. "I've brought you these." I nervously stepped into the house to put the buns down in what looked like the kitchen area. I realised that I had not actually been invited in. The old man hadn't moved the whole time.

"Right, well, I'll leave you to it. You've probably got a lot to do." I said and left, cringing at my lack of composure. I was cursing myself all the way back down the track towards home.

When I told Chuey what had happened he gave an even bigger laugh than he had before. I said I thought I'd take more buns next week. Chuey was smiling as he nodded and said that he thought that was a good idea too.

The next time I set off for the walk up to the old man's house it seemed to take much less time. I arrived at the old man's house and again I tentatively knocked on the door. Again there was no answer, so again I pushed the door open and there sat the old man just as before. This time I was prepared. I entered and put the buns in the same place. I asked him if there was anything he wanted help with while I was there. No answer. I could see a few crumbs around the kitchen area so I offered to sweep up for him. No answer. I could see a broom in the corner so I decided to do it anyway.

While I swept I kept up a jolly monologue, thinking that the old man must get lonely up there on his own all the time. I chatted about the weather and the poor harvest. He remained perfectly silent, but I didn't feel he was resenting my intrusion. I remember wondering why Confucius was so keen to visit this old man.

The trips up to the old man became part of my weekly routine. While I was there I would sweep up the crumbs or do whatever else was needed. All the time I kept up my one-sided conversation and all the time the old man maintained his silence. Then one day I was talking about Mo and the lads, telling him of an argument they had been having about the styles of government they favoured. Suddenly I heard him say, "Leading the people is like cooking small fish."

I jumped, startled by the unexpected sound. I looked round, but the old man was just sitting there with the same blank expression. Not sure what to say, I asked if he would like some small fish brought up next time Chuey caught some. There was no response. He just sat there, quite still.

I had started to think that I might have imagined the old man's strange comment about small fish, but then a similar thing happened a couple of weeks later. I realised that I hadn't told him that I was related to Confucius, so I said brightly, "Oh, you know Confucius, the scholar who comes to visit you, well he's my cousin."

I hoped that might prompt some reaction but I was not ready for the response which came. "Destroy the sage, banish wisdom and the whole world will have great order."

This time I actually saw him speak the words. He spoke with hardly a movement of his mouth and without any flicker of emotion. I waited for more but he just sat there, as still as before, so in the end I carried on with the sweeping, smiling to myself. When I had finished I bid him my usual cheery goodbye and left, thinking, 'Strange old man!' I wondered what he would have been like in his youth.

The movement of the Tao
By contraries proceeds;
And weakness marks the course
Of Tao's mighty deeds.

TAO TE CHING CHAPTER 40

10. DEPRESSION

I don't like to think I was ever a nag exactly, but I suppose I was often quite persistent in reminding Chuey about our family's needs. The more time he spent philosophising with his visitors, the less time he spent getting food. It was very frustrating, and I didn't mind telling him how I felt. Not that it did much good. Chuey seemed quite oblivious to my chiding. He always remained happy. I didn't know anyone else who managed to stay so content, but one day that changed.

The day before, a couple of scholars had arrived and stayed for most of the day, taking up Chuey's time. I was disappointed to see them returning early the next day. When I left to go to the market they were all in deep conversation, discussing the difference between the *that's it that deems* and the *that's it that goes by circumstance.* At the market I traded our few dried fish for barely enough provisions for a day let alone a week. I arrived home to find Chuey and his visitors still discussing the difference between the *that's it that deems* and the *that's it that goes by circumstance*. I interrupted their debate to tell Chuey that we didn't have any food for the children's dinner and that he needed to go and get some. The visitors left soon after, followed by Chuey with his bow.

Chuey returned while I was preparing our few vegetables for the evening meal. I was expecting him to at least bring back something for dinner and was annoyed that he arrived empty handed. It would be a thin, tasteless vegetable soup yet again and I let him know how disappointed I was. This time there were no clever excuses. Chuey just slumped down on the mat, staring into the fire. He barely touched his dinner. He didn't play with the children, but just sat there. The next morning he was the same and I realised that his mood had changed. For the first time in our married life, Chuey seemed to be depressed.

At first I assumed that my own frustrations had finally got through to him and that all my badgering had started to have some effect. I thought about what I had said when he had arrived home with no meat that night, but each time I recalled the conversation I found nothing to reproach myself for. In fact, I felt that I had every right to have been even more expressive about how annoyed I was with all the time he wasted.

When Chuey's depressed mood continued the next day, and the next, I started to see that the problem went deeper than that one night's meatless meal. Even then, part of me was happy to think that Chuey was coming to his senses at last, and that he had brought this upon himself with all his philosophising.

Chuey's friends couldn't help. Even Euan failed to lift his gloom. When visitors arrived, Chuey wasn't even polite. He would just shake his head, waft them away with his hand and sigh again. I had thought Chuey had been useless before, but as the weeks passed I could see this was now much worse. The new depressed Chuey could hardly find the energy to stand up, let alone empty and reset the fish traps. It was hard on the children. It was hard on me.

Then, after three months of Chuey's moping, just as I was getting used to having a depressed husband, I heard Chuey outside chuckling to himself. "Oh my teacher, oh my teacher!" he kept repeating. And Chuey was back.

At first I was relieved, but then Chuey's explanation left me speechless. He told me that his depression had been caused by an incident which had occurred that day, while he had been out hunting with his bow. He had gone to the crown lands hoping to poach a duck or two, but then he had seen a jackdaw. It was no ordinary jackdaw. It had been a huge bird, with a wingspan of seven feet and eyes over an inch wide. The gigantic bird had almost flown straight into him. Chuey needed to duck down out of its way, the bird brushing his forehead as it passed. He was amazed that it had not seen him, especially with such big eyes.

The bird landed in a tree and Chuey decided to follow with his bow ready, thinking he would take a pot-shot at it. But as Chuey hurried after the bird he saw a grass-hopper sitting in a nice shady spot without a thought for its own safety. Then he saw a praying-mantis which was about to stretch forth its pincers to seize the grass-hopper but, just as it did, the giant jackdaw swooped down and swept-up both grass-hopper and praying-mantis in its huge beak. Chuey was there with his bow, well positioned to shoot. Instead he decided to take pity on the sad procession of carnage and put his bow away. However, just at that moment the game-keeper appeared and Chuey only just managed to get away in time.

I knew his brush with the law wouldn't have caused Chuey much worry. I had heard him laugh about much worse incidents than that. He tried to explain why it had been so important to him. He said he had taken it as a lesson. He said that before the incident with the giant jackdaw he had been 'looking into a murky pool thinking it was clear'. The grass-hopper and the praying mantis, then the jackdaw, himself and the game-keeper, were enough to show him that his pool was still murky. That was why it had affected him so badly.

When Chuey finished explaining his depression, I was left seething. After spending months repeatedly justifying my own role, and proving my innocence to myself time and time again, all my imagined defences went unchallenged. They were all totally irrelevant. I had played no part in his unhappiness at all. It wasn't my pushing, or our family's lack of food, that had troubled him, he was only bothered about his own 'murky pool'. As Chuey bounced back to his full vigorous self I found myself even more resentful of his inconsiderate levels of contentment. What right had he to be happy when we were living in such poverty? I could see that rather than moving forward, he was now more deeply entrenched in his ideas than ever.

With all of my frustrations, I began to find that Chuey's philosophising made me almost unbearably angry. It didn't help that the borders with the neighbouring country had been re-opened, with even more scholars dropping in to take Chuey away from his sandal making and fishing, only to discuss this thing which didn't exist, and which didn't not-exist either. The merest mention of the Tao would set my blood boiling.

I still loved Chuey. I would look at him with an aching emptiness, yearning for it to be like it had been at the start of our marriage. But time had moved on, and Chuey had not.

11. TEACHING

After Chuey turned down the Prime Minister's job I was dreading Cousin Confucius's next visit. I feared he might take it very badly that Chuey had been offered, and had refused, the one thing that he most wanted. I needn't have worried. When Confucius next arrived he was in very high spirits and he soon told us why. He had heard that two of the town's young men, Mensa and Hussain, wanted to study under him. I was amazed at the news, but I'm sure Yan would have recommended my cousin's teaching methods highly. That visit was the first time that Yan was not with him. The children were disappointed that Uncle Yan hadn't come, but it wasn't a surprise. On their previous visit we had heard that Yan was planning to go off out into the world to share his master's wisdom.

Early on the morning after Confucius's arrival, Mensa and Hussain knocked on our door. I had been eavesdropping on their conversations at the inn for years so I felt I knew them well, but it was something of a shock to have them visit. The sleeping mats had not been put away and the house was in a state, as usual. I knew their parents were fairly wealthy and I could only imagine what the lads would be thinking of our tiny cluttered home.

Confucius put his new students to work immediately, clearing the mats and making space. He kept up a constant stream of advice as they tackled the task. I stood there, waiting for the right moment to have a word with my cousin as it became clear that he was about to use our house as his schoolroom. In the end I gave up trying to stop the inevitable and went to get on with some jobs outside. When I heard Confucius telling my children, in their own home, to go and play outside, I had to go to the ancestor shrine to calm myself down.

When I came out of the shrine, I could see that the two older children had put a log under the window and were standing on it so they could peer through the cracks in the shutters. I quietly joined them and together we silently spied on our guests.

Mensa was holding our broom while Confucius looked on. "No no no, Mensa! This sceptre has the weight of regal authority. Let me show you," said Confucius, taking the broom. Instantly his body bent with the heavy weight. His face dropped into a strange weary expression. He glanced around, looking very worried, and took a couple of steps, dragging his feet as though he could hardly lift them. He also made a strange rasping sound as he took gulps of breath. The children laughed and I put my fingers to their mouths, while trying not to laugh myself. "Now try again, and remember the weight."

Mensa looked a bit apprehensive but took the broom and tried to emulate his new master. "Good

Mensa, good! But remember the breathing! You dare not breathe, remember. You dare not breathe!" Mensa tried to do the breathing, sounding quite ill, but Confucius had spotted another issue. "No! no! You're holding it too high!" exclaimed Confucius, taking back the symbol of royal authority. "Watch," he commanded, resuming his heavily burdened posture, expression and breathing, and explained, "Never higher than the position of the hands when making a bow, never lower than the position of the hands when giving a gift". He lifted and lowered the broom to demonstrate the acceptable limits on the height at which a sceptre might be held. "Alright, Hussain's turn."

I ushered the children away from the window, feeling that it was perhaps unlikely they would ever need to know the right way to hold a sceptre, and we left our guests to their studies.

At the end of the school day I heard Confucius telling Mensa and Hussain that they wouldn't be able to continue their education the next day as he had to leave on royal business, but that he hoped to return soon and they would continue where they had left off. I didn't know if Confucius's planned departure had been influenced by the lecture I had given him the previous day. I had plainly informed him of the state of our family's finances and, more importantly, the emptiness of our larder. I had delivered the speech with my very real anxiety showing and there was no way he could have missed my pointed reference to the difference between a mother's duty to her children compared to her cousins. Cousin Confucius was always very keen on being partial to one's closest relatives.

The next day I left Confucius with the children as I set off to do the washing. At the slabs, I leaned over to Sue to tell her that Mensa and Hussain had started studying under Confucius. I had whispered the news as the lads were already at their usual table. I was hoping to hear their impressions of their first lesson, but I didn't have the chance. The king's carriage had just driven into the square.

The king's visits had become almost regular. Since his first visit, when the wheelwright had so bravely escaped with his life, the king had stopped by several times. Each time he had taken tea at the inn before carrying on along his way. Some said that the tea was his only reason for stopping, or more likely the serving of the tea, in the form of Kim who was growing up to be an extremely attractive young woman.

I had missed all of the king's previous visits, but I had heard many reports. The town always buzzed with accounts of each visit for weeks after. I had particularly enjoyed hearing about the previous royal visit as it involved a friend of ours, the butcher.

On that occasion the king had happened to arrive on a market day and had been surprised to find the usually quiet little town so busy. In the hurly-burly of business it took a while for anyone to notice the royal visitor and the king apparently decided to enjoy his brief moment of anonymity. He strolled over to a group of people in the corner of the square. He must have assumed it to be some sort of street entertainment to attract such an audience. Anyone from the town would have known what was happening, but the king would have been surprised to find that they were watching the butcher.

People soon sensed the royal presence and there were frantic bows as the fearful subjects backed away from their majestic ruler. Only the butcher remained unaware of the new spectator. With his back to the royal arrival, engrossed in his work, he carried on cutting up the ox. After a large chunk of meat had fallen to the ground the butcher stepped back and paused. The king said, "Bravo," at which the butcher turned to see who was applauding his work.

He gave a little bow and said, "Thank you Your Majesty."

"So tell me my good man, how did you come to be so proficient with that knife of yours? Your skill is most excellent," said the king in his regal tones.

"Well," said the butcher in his slow, rustic accent, wiping his hands on his apron and approaching the king, "I would not want to correct Your Majesty, but I left skill behind a while back. It is true that I used to work hard at my skills, but now your humble servant has found a way which is far better than any skill could ever be."

"Oh," said the king, who had perhaps not expected such a talkative butcher. The butcher carried on.

"When I first started as a butcher, all I saw was the ox. But after three years I learned not to see a whole ox. Nowadays I don't look with the eye at all. Now I look with the mind, and I see the natural lines. Then it is easy. My knife glides through the crevices, making use of the cavities, with my job merely to let my knife take advantage of what is already there. In that way I miss the sinews and especially the bones. A good butcher changes his knife each year because he slices. An ordinary butcher needs to change knives each month because he hacks. Now, this knife, I've been using it for nineteen years! It has seen-off thousands of oxen, but feel that."

He offered the edge of the knife to the king, who politely removed his glove, tentatively touched the metal and nodded.

"Sharp as if it had just been sharpened, eh?"

More royal nodding.

"You see, between the joints there are spaces, and the blade's edge has no real thickness." With that the butcher slipped his knife back into the hanging carcass and moved it smoothly through the flesh, cutting while he talked. "Once you understand that, then there is plenty of room for a knife to work its way through. I should just say, however, if I come to a complicated part, and I can see there will be some difficulty, then I have to be careful." The butcher had slowed the knife until the blade was barely moving. "You see, with great attention I move my hand, slowly, until…" , whump, another joint of meat dropped to the ground like a great sod of earth and the butcher stood back triumphantly.

The king nodded his head in appreciation of the speech and demonstration, then in kingly fashion he raised his hand for silence and proclaimed, "Excellent, my fine butcher. You have told me about butchering an ox, but I have heard words which tell me how to live life fully."

The butcher was greatly surprised at such high praise, and had a broad smile as the king patted him on the back warmly. Some people say that the king then grimaced slightly as he delicately picked a morsel of meat from his elegant glove, which he then took several attempts to flick off the elegant glove on his other hand.

I had enjoyed the accounts of the king's previous visits so I was excited to see His Royal Highness with my own eyes. As he stepped down from his coach I was impressed. He looked properly regal, complete with a sumptuous fur-edged cloak. There was no mistaking his rank, which was reassuring after my embarrassment at mistaking his son, the prince, for a scholar.

I thought that the king looked disappointed to find the square empty compared to his previous visit, without the bustle of market-day, just a quiet little town square once more. I wasn't sure what to do in the royal presence, but all the other women just carried on washing in a half-hearted fashion, far more interested in the royal show than in their dirty clothes.

The king walked to his usual table and Kim came out to take his royal order. "What, no wheelwright, no butcher today? Well then who's going to teach me how to run my country?"

The king had clearly meant this as a joke, but Kim innocently offered, "I think you'll find the young gentlemen at the table at the back there will more than meet your needs, Majesty," her humble voice sounding like her quaint little bob of a bow.

"Excellent," said the king, who had obviously come to regard our town as a source of entertainment. "Approach the royal table," he commanded. "Come on lads, don't be shy, I'm only the king," he bellowed, turning to check that Kim had noticed his little jest.

The lads looked at each other, perhaps remembering that the wheelwright had been fortunate to escape with his life from such an encounter. They shuffled forward, bowed, then just stood there, unsure of what regal etiquette demanded next. The king seemed unconcerned about such matters. "So, who wants to give me the first lesson? You, the tall one. What's yer name?" He raised the royal glove towards Mensa.

"Mensa, Your Majesty." He looked nervous and clasped his hands together tightly, but began well and sounded just how we all imagined a royal advisor ought to sound. "If I were to presume to give Your Majesty a lesson, Your Majesty, it would be on benevolence and righteousness, and the ways of the sage-kings of old."

"Ah, well I like to think that I am already a benevolent and righteous ruler, but there's always room for improvement. If it will help to make me more benevolent I suppose I should hear your lesson. Pray continue," said the king, who glanced round at Kim, as if to check she had noticed his cheerily benevolent manner. He could not have taken her smile as anything other than encouragement.

As Mensa began to describe the benefits of benevolence and righteousness there was a distraction in the middle of the square. It was Joe. He had started running around, shouting out that everyone ought to emigrate quickly if the king was about to start practicing benevolence. In his best 'mad' voice he raved that it would end up with people eating each other raw!

Luckily the king, like most people, took no notice of Joe's mad rantings. A quick glance was enough to tell him that it was just some lunatic fellow whom it was quite beneath his dignity to punish. I breathed a sigh of relief, thinking to myself that one day Joe would push his luck too far.

Mensa didn't have the presence of mind to pause until after the distraction had passed. He was already part of the way through his ponderous description of the benefits of benevolence and righteousness before the royal attention had returned to him. When it did, it seems that it found a topic the king was not particularly fond of.

The king wearily raised his hand to interrupt Mensa's speech. "Yes, on second thoughts, I think I might have heard that lesson once or twice before. Maybe later." He gave a flick of his glove as if wafting Mensa out of his presence.

"What about you?" he said pointing at Hussain.

"I am afraid that my lesson might be rather similar, Your Majesty," said Hussain, sounding quite literally afraid.

"Oh," said the king disappointedly, sadly adding, "I had come to expect more from this little town, I must say."

But then, without waiting for the royal invitation, Mo said brightly, "If I were to give Your Majesty a lesson, it would be on Universal Love."

"Oh!" enthused the king, glad to find that not all of the town's royal advisors were of the same persuasion. "We will hear your lesson on Universal Love."

Sue and I exchanged looks of dread. We had already heard Mo's dour deliberations on that topic.

After his initial brightness, Mo set off on his usual justification of everyone loving everyone else. The king, however, was more fortunate than most of us. He had the authority and he decided to wield it. It wasn't long before he held up his hand to stop Mo's logical, though somewhat lengthy, justification of his beloved universal love. "Fascinating theory ..."

"But, Your Majesty, it's not just a theory. The sage-kings of old ..."

"Yes, yes yes ..."

"But if a ruler, like yourself, could be persuaded to ..."

"Yes yes, but I think I get the gist of it!" said the king with some weight, which even Mo was forced to accept. The king seemed to be boring of the game. It was with fading interest that he said to Ian, "How 'bout you? How would you have me run my domain?"

Ian spoke clearly, and with confidence. "I think ruling the kingdom would be as easy as rolling a marble around in your palm, Your Majesty."

The king sat up with surprise at the boldness of Ian's remark. "Well, I am sure it would be easy for one of your undoubted ability, but do you have any advice for one with such humble gifts as myself?" There was an edge to the king's words which invited caution and everyone held their breath.

Ian replied, without seeming at all worried. "Have you ever seen a shepherd drive a flock of a hundred sheep? He merely walks peacefully behind, letting the sheep go where they will. What easier way could there be to rule a kingdom? That is how I would do it, Your Majesty."

Ian had spoken without any indication that he was joking, but the king seemed happy to interpret his remarks as a joke, which was probably just as well. Everyone breathed a sigh of relief when the king said laughingly, "Well young man, should you choose to swallow that medicine yourself, I wish you luck! You might find that even ruling your own home in such a careless fashion is not quite as easy as you imagine!" There was polite laughter at the king's jesting, but then the air of tension returned as the king looked at Hans expectantly, waiting for his next piece of advice now that the game had become fun again.

Hans started trying to mouth something, but his stutter stopped the words coming out.

"Well come on lad, out with it!" snapped the king, who was obviously not accustomed to having to wait for his advisors' pearls of wisdom.

Then, almost miraculously it seemed to us who knew his usual problems, Hans managed to say, "Mm, may I present this to Your m-Majesty." And with that he reached into his bag and produced a book.

The king was as surprised as everyone else, and leaned back as though wary of the unexpected gift. He received the book with a look of mild disdain, thinly disguised as gratitude. It was only after noting Kim's eager expression that he looked at it.

He was politely pretending to find the book interesting, but then started to read one part with real attention. He laughed, then read out loud, "If a kingdom believes in lucky times, or serves ghosts and spirits, or if it puts its trust in divination and loves sacrifices it will surely decay." I saw Mo and Mensa swap astonished looks, and both glared at Hans. The king carried on reading and was clearly highly amused by what he was reading.

"And this bit is good. Listen to this. 'The Five Vermin of the State. Number One: Scholars who praise the ways of former kings, thus casting doubt upon the laws of the time and causing the ruler to be of two minds'. Ha! That is so true!"

The king was laughing to himself, clearly enjoying what he was reading. He looked at Hans. "Did you write this? It's great!"

"Yes" came the almost instant reply. Mo, Mensa and Hussain looked at each other with a mixture of belligerence and bewilderment. Ian was as surprised as the others but seemed to find it all highly amusing.

The king was still reading, and had found another part which he felt the need to share. "Oh yes, this is priceless! 'Talking about beauty does not make you beautiful. Talking about benevolence and righteousness won't order your state'. This is tremendous stuff! Thank you young man I will certainly enjoy reading that. And, mark my words, there are a few people at court who I will be *ordering* to read it!" The king was clearly tickled at what he had been given to read. "What's your name?"

"H–Hans, Your M–Majesty."

"Good. Well done." And turning to Kim, he said "And thank you for your suggestion. Your young men make splendid advisors. And once again, this little town has provided me with yet more excellent service. Why, I'm coming to believe that every last man, woman and child of you must be a philosopher! What! Hey!?" Still laughing at his own joke, the king took a sip of his tea.

Just at that moment, Confucius walked into the square. On seeing the king, he stopped, straightened his gown and belt and adjusted his hat. My heart sank as he then adopted a similar expression to the one he had worn at the funeral all those years ago and to the one he had recently been teaching to his new students. He also started to make the exaggerated wheezing sound. Once his features had been suitably contorted, he suddenly zoomed forwards towards the king, stopping abruptly just in front of him. The king recoiled visibly. Confucius then made a deep bow.

While Confucius was still bowing, the king stood up, clearly now in a rush to leave. "Right, thank you all," he said hurriedly. "No time for any more lessons today. Be seeing you." He took a quick gulp of his tea and gave another nod in Kim's direction before walking briskly towards his carriage, glancing back to check that he had made a clean getaway.

A desperate sounding Confucius called out after the king, "But Your Highness, I must speak to you about benevolence and righteousness and the ways of the sage-kings of old."

"Sorry, the lads have already told me all about it," replied the king, without even bothering to turn his head. "See you all next time," he called out as he climbed into his carriage. Then the carriage pulled off, the royal glove giving its royal wave as the coach drove off out of the square.

Confucius stood there dejected. He pulled off his hat and let his pious expression relax, allowing his face to return to something like normal.

12. HARD TIMES

Finding enough food for our growing family was always an issue, but when the rains failed for two years things became desperate. My heart would ache as I divided up the available food each mealtime, trying to decide which bowl needed each morsel most. It wasn't just our family who were suffering. Even after receiving advice from all five of the town's young philosophers, the king didn't manage to make life any better for his subjects. Times became hard for everyone. One year there was a smaller pot of honey for winning the fencing contest and the following year there was no honey at all, just a wooden plaque.

Taxes were increased yet again to pay for the seemingly endless war, but people simply had no more to give. Then the taxes paled into insignificance when the army requisitions started. Sometimes when the soldiers came to gather supplies it wasn't even clear which side we were supporting. They could have been members of Robber Chih's gang for all we knew. Not that you tried to stop armed men from taking your last grains of rice.

Many people left the town at that time and others simply died. In those days, keeping up with the neighbours was easy and hunger was almost universal. If the king had dared to visit in those dark times he would not have received much of a welcome. The people's hunger would have spoken for them. There was a lot of resentment towards the ruler. Perhaps that is why he preferred to stay locked up in his palace, indulging his passion for watching sporting contests.

Our own family fared better than most as we were already used to scraping a living in hard times, though the fish became scarcer as people's hunger turned them to fishing, but blinded them to any thoughts of conserving the stocks. Chuey would return to his fish traps to find them emptied and discarded on the bank, or simply vanished. He needed to travel further to find the fish, and even then it was common for him to return with little to eat. Chuey's sandal business was an early casualty of those hungry years.

Not all of us were starving though. Dan's arrow-making business had continued to grow and he had become quite grand. Sue had stopped washing with us when some of the other women had made no attempt to hide their resentment at her new-found wealth. Even before then, I had learned to avoid asking Sue about the business, especially the level of wages that Dan paid to his workers. There wasn't much humour around in those days.

Other people to prosper were the town officials who continued to gain weight while the rest of us grew thinner. I used to try to imagine how we might have been living if Chuey had accepted the 'job offer'. It was a desperate feeling, looking at the few grains in the steaming pot, then at the children's glum faces.

It was in those hard years that the merchant told me some startling news about Leah and her husband. Apparently one of their visitors, a foreign scholar, had told the king, "Here is a man who looks as if he has the Tao and yet he is starving." He suggested it was something of a disgrace for the country to allow such men to starve, so the king had sent an official with a large bag of rice. Leah's husband greeted the official with bows but refused the gift. The official tried to persuade him to accept the rice but once more he politely refused, so the official left, taking the rice with him.

I can imagine Leah's reaction. Given her strong feelings and sharp tongue, I am sure her husband would have very soon regretted his decision. Leah had been quite scathing of Chuey's decision not to accept the job of prime minister but, at that time, an offer of rice seemed much more important than merely being offered the job of running the country. I heard later that Leah's husband had explained his actions by saying that the king did not know him, so if the next report he heard was unfavourable he might be just as likely to send a punishment. With a hungry family to feed, and with her belief that the family of a man of the Tao could expect comfort and happiness, I can imagine that Leah would have found her husband's refusal of sustenance very hard to accept.

As we suffered our own hungry distress such a decision sounded absurd. I fantasized that Chuey might himself receive a present from the prince, but no such gift arrived. Our situation became so bad that we agreed that Chuey should go to see the Marquis to ask for a loan of some rice. When he returned empty-handed it was a bitter blow. Chuey clearly felt the disappointment and almost apologetically recounted the details of the encounter.

Apparently the Marquis had initially received the request favourably, telling Chuey that he would be glad to help, saying, "I will be receiving the taxes from the people soon. What do you want, what shall we say, three hundred gold pieces? Will that be enough?"

Chuey had been angry at the offer and had told the Marquis, "As I journeyed here yesterday I heard a voice calling me. When I looked around I saw it was coming from a small fish trapped in a puddle in one of the ruts in the road. I asked the fish what he was doing there and he told me he was an exile from the Eastern Ocean and asked me politely if I had a peck-measure of water that I could let him have. I told him that I would be seeing you today but that tomorrow I would redirect the course of the Great Western river his way, and asked him if that would do. At that the fish flushed with anger and thundered that all it needed was a little water to survive but given my answer I should look for him the next day on the dried fish stall!"

When Chuey had finished, I wept. In the most desperate of times, with his family literally starving,

Chuey had offended the man who has just offered him three hundred pieces of gold. I wondered how much rice 300 pieces of gold could buy. The incident left my spirits entirely broken. Finally I could agree wholeheartedly with Leah on the similarity of our husbands, and that we were both doomed.

In those black times there were few visitors coming to discuss the Tao with Chuey, but I remember one scholar calling. He wore a fine gown and his big belly clearly showed that he wasn't suffering from the famine. The scholar claimed that he had come to ask Chuey about some subtlety concerning the Tao, but after daintily quibbling over some minor intellectual point, he said, "I really must ask you, Chuey, about your Tao. I mean, look at you. Your clothes are of coarse material, and even then they are covered with patches. And your shoes are held together with string!" He gave a little laugh, as if to underline just how far removed his shoes were from Chuey's. "Why would someone in possession of the Tao, as you undoubtedly are Sir, find themselves in such distress?"

The sugar-sweet wording, with its false concern, wasn't enough to hide the scholar's enjoyment in asking the question, but Chuey answered as if it had been a genuine enquiry.

"Worn clothes and shoes held together with string are not distress. If one has the Tao and the Virtue but is unable to use them, then that is distress." He pointed to his ragged clothes. "These are merely known as 'not being around at the right time'. It is something like when monkeys move in the prickly mulberry or in thorny date trees. In such an environment, they move slowly with caution, quite unlike the animals one usually sees running and jumping around at ease in other trees."

The scholar seemed suitably chastened by Chuey's frank words, but he didn't seem to have enjoyed receiving the lesson and left soon after. I just remember thinking that 'not being around at the right time' felt like distress to me.

It was hard to continue making trips up to the old man during those bare times. I wouldn't have shared our family's inadequate resources except that I suppose I had come to see him as part of the family. Often, the pitiful morsel I carried up to him barely justified the trek but, even though weak with hunger myself, I still felt obliged to maintain the routine once I had started it.

As I cleaned his cottage I would carry on my one-sided conversation. For his sake I tried to keep it positive, though I imagine he also had to put up with a good deal of complaining, and every now and then I would hear him make one of his strange statements.

On one occasion I mentioned a rumour that had spread rapidly around the town that, due to the continual warring, the taxes were set to rise yet again. People were frightened and angry and there had even been talk of rebellion. I told the old man that I would be glad if they would finish the war once and for all, one way or another, so we could all get back to normal. Victory or defeat, I didn't mind. Then I heard him say, "A skilful commander strikes a decisive blow and stops. He does not dare to assert his complete mastery."

I turned and looked at him with a surprised smile. For the first time I had understood what he had meant and his comment had been both relevant and sensible. I was delighted at this breakthrough in communication. It made me wonder whether, perhaps, some of his other comments had been more than just the senile outbursts I had taken them to be. That idea was confirmed next time he spoke.

I had been telling him that I had heard the lads discussing the pros and cons of the current war. Mo had taken a much higher stance, saying that the number of deaths and the amount of suffering make any offensive war the most unrighteous act imaginable. I was saying that I agreed with Mo when the old man interrupted my speech with, "On occasions of festivity, to be on the left is the prized position, on occasions of mourning, the right hand. The Commander-In-Chief has his place on the right of the second in command, the positions arranged as the rites of mourning."

I stood and thought about his words for a moment. The link between the positions of soldiers and mourners made a poetic extension to Mo's views on war. I looked at him wondering if he would say more, but he remained silent, sitting as still and as upright as he always did. After that I started to take more notice of the old man's statements. I'd think about each one and I grew to value his strange little nuggets of wisdom.

The money I earned from potting was very important to the family at that time. Demand for the ordinary range of cups, bowls and plates had reduced but, strangely, the demand for our larger pieces grew. By then my pots had developed into elaborate creations. The potter had encouraged me in this direction as he had become keen on decorating them. At first he simply painted them with various colours of glaze, then he started to play with different patterns of indenting and even took to adorning them with metal. The resulting pots were considered fine, even by city standards, and a trader regularly took our best pieces there. I used to find it strange that people in the capital could be affording such luxury items while the rest of us were starving.

We desperately needed the extra coins that my fancy pots earned for us, but potting became much more than just a way of getting money. When the potter had first shown us the pottery, I hadn't thought much of his innovation of fixing a log onto the wheel so he could work without help. How that changed. The potter could only let me have one session a week as we were constrained by the kiln's capacity but once a week, working alone, I could escape to another world, drifting off into some daydream while I sat there mechanically fashioning pots. That brief island of calm became so vital for me that I'd get quite anxious if I thought I might have to miss a session for some reason.

It would be too embarrassing to say what I used to dream about while I sat at the potter's wheel, but at that time a new fantasy took hold. It started from something the old man said. I had been sweeping the old man's floor, talking about pottery and about how the pot seems to 'grow out of itself, almost by itself'. Then, as I carried on mindlessly giving him a full description of the process, he made one of his remarks. He said, "When the sage-king rules, after his work is completed, throughout the country everyone says it happened of its own accord." The old man's comment had only a passing relevance to what I had been talking about, but nevertheless it was another of his sayings which stuck in my mind.

The next time I was sitting at the potter's wheel I playfully imagined myself to be a sage-king of old, ruling the world of clay through my mystical wisdom.

It started as something of a joke but the fantasy grew to be much more than that. After sitting at the wheel, I would take a moment to summon the power. Then, proceeding through the familiar steps, I'd be ruling the clay revolving in my hands, as if by magic. The spinning clay, with its mysterious mixture of motion and stillness, became a world that I had total control over. I had the entire world in my hands as I allowed the pot to form. As the weeks passed, the fantasy evolved until I would fancy that I, the magical sage-king, would somehow actually 'become' the clay that I was transforming. In those moments I was totally absorbed in the potting. I would fully lose myself: there was no separation, no distinction between pot and potter. It almost felt as though I could feel myself to be the shape of the pot that was forming through the power of my will. And how I loved that power!

I wouldn't have thought much about my sage-king daydreams, but they had a big effect on my potting. I made much better pots when I was being a sage-king. I could emerge from a session at the wheel and be amazed by the elegance of the pot I had produced. After the potter had applied his artistic finishes and glazing, the pieces were truly beautiful. The agent said they were as fine as anything produced in the country and even started passing on some of the pieces to another agent who usually only dealt in bronzeware. The potter and I were never paid much for the pots ourselves, but in those days the money I earned from my potting sometimes almost felt like the difference between life and death.

A violent wind does not last for a whole morning; a sudden rain does not last for the whole day. To whom is it that these (two) things are owing? To Heaven and Earth. If Heaven and Earth cannot make such (spasmodic) actings last long, how much less can man!

TAO TE CHING CHAPTER 23

13. MUCH WORSE THAN JUST ANNOYING

After the rains finally returned, albeit with disastrous flooding, we suffered the hardest winter yet. It was a time when people had little energy to help themselves and it was hard to think of helping others, but the next summer marked the beginning of the end of the hungry years. With the aching hunger receding, the town slowly started to get back to something like its old self. Laughter started to reappear like flowers in spring, not just the empty gallows-humour we had grown used to, but real sunshine-happiness humour. Washing mornings began to be more fun again and there started to be more weddings than funerals.

It's strange how the mind works. Chuey had turned down the Prime Minister's job, we had suffered famine and flood and he had refused gold which could have given us food when it was most needed but, looking back, it was a discussion about fishes that somehow seems more important.

We hadn't seen Hue for a while as he had started a job in local government, administering a neighbouring province, but then he arrived unexpectedly one day. I had tutted to myself on hearing a carriage pull up. Chuey had only recently resumed making sandals and I was not at all pleased that yet another excuse had arrived to distract him. When I looked to see who had arrived, I was happily surprised. "Hue!" I exclaimed, calling to Chuey who was out the back. I went out to greet our old friend.

Hue seemed pleased to see me but his tone was a little too polite as he asked if Chuey was home. I responded by politely inviting him in. I asked him, a little awkwardly, if he would like some tea. Then Chuey came in with a great smile at seeing his dear old adversary again, but it was clear that something was wrong. Hue said, "Hello Chuey," without much warmth.

Chuey can talk his nonsense all day and all night too, but he can talk directly enough when he wants. He said simply, "Well Hue, what is it?"

With a hint of animosity Hue demanded, "Chuey, what's this about you wanting my job?"

Chuey and I both laughed at the question. Hue maintained his accusing manner and said that he had heard a rumour that someone was plotting to displace him in his new job and that someone else had heard another rumour that the mysterious plotter might be Chuey. By the time Hue had finished making his case against his dear friend, and seeing our amusement at the accusation, he had already started to join in our laughter at the ridiculous suspicions.

Chuey walked up to Hue and clamped his arm round his shoulder. In a dramatic tone said, "Have you heard, my friend, about the sacred Phoenix that lives in the South?" He used his hands to accompany his words with elaborate gestures, as if he were telling a story to the children. "It arises out of the south sea and flies to the sea in the north. It never alights but on the sacred begonia tree. It will eat nothing except the most exquisite rare fruits and will drink nothing but water from the sweetest, purest springs. One day there was an owl hunched over his dinner, which was a half-rotten old rat carcass. The owl saw the Phoenix flying over. He screeched in panicked alarm and clutched the chewed-up, festering rat to himself in fear and dismay." Chuey patted his friend on the back, grinning. "No my friend, whoever it is who wants your festering job, it's certainly not me."

Hue seemed very happy and very relieved. "Of course, I didn't really think that you …" he started, but Chuey waved away his explanation and we continued in a much friendlier mood.

After drinking their tea, the two men went out for a stroll. When they returned it was obvious that they had completely returned to normal, engaged in discussion as usual.

"No, sorry Chuey, no! There is no way that you can know what goes on in a fish's head! I'm not you, so I can't know what is going on in your head. You are not a fish, so you obviously cannot know what is going on in a fish's head. Come on! Admit it, you're wrong this time."

I smiled at Hue's happy, triumphant, challenging tone. It was good to hear him mounting yet another attack, just like the good old days. I put the water on for another round of tea.

When the tea was made and delivered to the two combatants, the conversation had still not progressed. I asked them what they were talking about. It was rare for me to intervene in their fencing matches, but this one sounded more interesting than usual and I had missed the start of it.

Hue explained that they had been on the other side of town, standing by the river. Apparently Chuey had said, "Look at them darting around. That's what fish enjoy."

Hue had seen in Chuey's remark a chink of weakness and with it the chance of an attack. "You're not a fish! How do you know what makes a fish happy?"

Hue described how the discussion had continued from there and concluded his account by saying, "And now he won't admit he's wrong!" He sounded like one of the children, appealing to me if one of the others was being unreasonable. I had to admit Hue had a point. I had heard enough of the subsequent battle to know that Chuey was not having it all his own way for once. But he wasn't finished yet.

"Hue, Let's go back to your original question. You said 'How do you know what makes fish happy?' The terms of your question clearly show that you already know that I know what makes fish happy."

And they were off again, cutting and thrusting, parrying and riposting. When they eventually grew bored of each other's intransigence it was time to change the conversation, but Hue couldn't let it go. He turned to me and whined, "He's wrong, and he won't admit it!"

I smiled, and said that I thought they were both being silly, but inside I couldn't help agreeing with Hue. As far as I was concerned Hue had scored a hit. He had finally won a debate, though Chuey was as serene as ever. With a little shake of his head and a smile he said, "Well, I know what I know."

Why was it so important to me that Chuey had finally been proved wrong? I had heard Chuey say things which I had not agreed with, and I had heard him admit that his ideas were useless, but I had never before heard him defeated. After Hue had gone I pondered the exchange. Hue had beaten him and the worst part was that Chuey's only response had been a weak play on words. If Chuey had sportingly admitted the hit, as I had seen him do many times when fencing, I am sure I wouldn't have taken the discussion on fishes' happiness so badly but that day, it seemed to me, I had seen that Chuey could not back down. It mattered because I had finally come to see that Chuey would never move on from his useless ideas. It seemed to me that even though Chuey had won all the previous battles, with one little triumph Hue had actually won the war. All of Chuey's victories were just hot air compared to his friend's grasp on reality. Until then I suppose part of me had always clung to the idea that Chuey would eventually come good and that his approach would be proved right. It is funny that a silly discussion about the happiness of fish should colour my view of my husband to that extent, but that is what happened.

My patience with Chuey's visitors and all the philosophising had worn out, but I did hear one discussion which raised my interest. A visiting scholar was discussing some point or other when he happened to mention a sage who he reverentially referred to as 'The Transcendent Master of the Void'. Apparently this great mystic could fly for fifteen days at a time, travelling on the winds to the very edge of space. As his description continued I nearly dropped the cups when I realised he was talking about Leah's husband. I listened for more clues but none came.

After the scholar left I asked Chuey whether he had heard about Leah's husband's flying. He just laughed and said, "It must be nice for him to be able to save his legs." He came and stood behind me and started to massage my shoulders, but I shook him off and persisted with the conversation. Only then did he make a serious comment, saying, "Only fifteen days? And after the fifteen days, where does he go back to?"

How long he flew for and where he flew back to afterwards seemed irrelevant. To me it all sounded like nonsense.

By then I was extremely annoyed with the Tao, which apparently neither exists nor does it 'not exist'. Then I heard Chuey telling someone that the Tao 'effaces the actions of bad men'. So, this Tao is not even claiming to be 'good'. Chuey said that even Robber Chih has the Tao.

As well as the endless discussions on the Tao, I was forced to endure such useless debates as whether there was a 'cause' of the whole world or whether there was not a 'cause' of the whole world. I would sit angrily spinning through these discussions, not for enjoyment as I had once done, but purely trying to put clothes on my children's backs.

Once I saw that Chuey would not accept that he had been wrong about the happy fishes I saw that none of it would ever change. The children would never have any better clothes, let alone Chuey and I. We would never have a house which was big enough for the family to live in comfortably and, even though food wasn't such a problem by then, there were still plenty of ordinary items we could not afford.

After Chuey and Hue's discussion on the happiness of fishes, my resentment at Chuey's philosophising grew even stronger. I felt I had been conned. I resented the Duke who had praised Chuey so highly, I resented Leah for telling me that our husbands' Tao would bring us comfort and ease, but most of all I cursed myself for failing to heed my parents' reservations about Chuey's suitability as a husband.

One time, in my desperation, I tried to suggest that Chuey write his ideas down in a book, or that he should start a 'school of Tao'. He just started telling me another one of his stories. He said that once upon a time there had been three kings. The king of the North was Act-on-a-hunch, the king of the South was Act-in-a-flash and the king of the place between was No-form. Chuey said that the kings of the North and South often travelled to meet in No-form's kingdom where he treated them well. They found this helpful and thought they should show some appreciation for their neighbour's hospitality. They noticed that unlike other men he had no openings for seeing, hearing, eating and so on. So they decided that they would make some openings for him. They made one a day, but after seven days their friend lay dead. At the end of his story Chuey was silent.

It was late and I was too weary to argue about it. I just thought, 'What is that supposed to mean? He sounds like the old man.'

Chuey must have read my mind because he then said, "I once heard the old man say that to organise is to destroy."

I didn't even say goodnight.

It was clear that Chuey and I were on different paths. Nothing showed this more than when our youngest child became gravely ill. A cough had been going round the town which for some reason mainly affected the children. At first it seemed like any of the other coughs and colds that get passed around during the colder months as we huddled together indoors. We soon understood that this was a much more fearful foe when one of the youngsters in the town died.

A child's funeral is a terrible thing at the best of times, but watching the tiny coffin pass while your own children are under the threat of the same disease is indescribably distressing. After more deaths in the town there was a general feeling of panic, particularly amongst families with young children. By the time we learned that the mild, snuffly cough was actually a killer, three of our children were already sick with it and it seemed that I was about to lose all of my little ones.

We arranged the sick children around the fireplace. I tended to the sick ones while Chuey kept the other two well away, sleeping out in the lean-to shed at the back of the extension. It was a terrible time, watching the children suffer as the coughing took a hold. Starting as dry little throat clearings, the intensity grew over a period of days into terrible fits, with the children coughing with such terrible force that it seemed that they must surely cough their lungs up. As the disease progressed, it seemed to be strangling each of my children in front of me, the violence of the cough given a pitiful echo in the heartbreaking sound as they struggled to suck in another breath, to once more cough out again with such destructive force.

Eventually they would cough themselves sick, vomiting up whatever small amount of food I had managed to coax them to eat. The violence of the coughing fits and the sheer exhaustion afterwards were painful to behold. All I could do was to watch helplessly, knowing that this disease had already claimed other young lives.

Gradually the fits of two of the children started to lessen. They ate more, they slept more and began to look more healthy. Their recovery was a huge relief but the youngest was not getting any better. As the other children started to regain strength and began to look well, she declined further. It was as though fate had allowed me to keep the others but only on the condition that it would take the one. That was a deal I could not possibly allow.

The youngest had always been a weak child. Suffering the worst winter of the famine at the tenderest of ages had left her frail. She was still only tiny when the coughing arrived and as I held her little body it seemed almost inevitable that she would succumb, a thought which made me desperate with dread. Once the other children were well enough to be up, saving my little girl became my only focus.

The coughing fits always seemed worse at night. Perhaps it was the cold or perhaps it was the lying down which triggered the terrible cascades. If lying down was a problem then she would have to be held. If cold was a problem then she would be held by the fire. I sat by the fire with my little one on my knee for days at a time.

We heard that one of the families in the town had found that getting the sick child to inhale steam had helped ease the breathing and had lessened the severity of the coughing fits. We tried to arrange bowls of hot water close to her face, but with our little one being so small it was difficult. After several failed attempts, Chuey came up with a larger arrangement. He used sheets to form a tent-like structure close to the fire. A bamboo pipe brought steam from a closed pot to the tent, keeping it filled with a warm cloud. We kept the sheets damp to keep in the steam, hoping this would also help to stop the disease spreading to the other children. The 'steam-tent' worked well and that sweaty space became my whole world as I fought to save my child.

There was a lot of time to think as I sat in there. Most of my thinking was on one question. 'Why couldn't we afford to call the doctor?' Each time her weak little body convulsed its way through another fit of coughing, with me crying, sure that this time I was losing my little one, my thoughts would again turn to asking why it was that we couldn't call on professional medical help. I asked Chuey whether there was any way at all in which we might be able to afford the doctor's help. He just asked what I thought the doctor might be able to do.

Chuey had always doubted doctors. I remember one time he had been discussing the illness of one of his friends. The friend had not been short of money but when he fell ill he didn't call a doctor and even stopped his family from calling one. When his condition worsened the family decided to disregard his instruction and three doctors were summoned. The man wasn't pleased but allowed the doctors to examine him.

The first doctor emerged from the examination saying the illness was grave but curable. He prescribed various remedies, convinced they would work. The sick man had said, "This man merely recites the clap-trap from the books. Send him away without further ado!"

The second doctor reported that the man's illness was due to taking too much milk at his mother's breast and that it was too late to effect a full cure. The man preferred this pronouncement and said, "This one speaks well. Invite him to dinner."

The third doctor merely shook his head and said, "The time approaches, as it does for everyone. No medicine can do anything for you." The sick man was delighted saying, "This one has spirit! We should pay him generously." The man took no medicine but made a full recovery.

We had heard that tale in happier times and had laughed at the happy outcome, but as I thought back to that slice of so-called wisdom while nursing my little girl, my mind turned blacker and blacker as I realised that it was just that sort of thinking that could cost the life of my child. How I would have loved to have had that first doctor come and deliver his 'clap-trap from the books', but we had no money for doctors. We could barely feed ourselves. As I sat there in the steam, it seemed to me that Chuey's easy-going way was responsible for my little one's terrible suffering. With each weak, tortured cough and with each pitiful sucking-in of breath, my resentment at Chuey's useless philosophising hardened.

I stayed in that steamy tent night and day for what seemed like an eternity. I did however leave my sick girl with Chuey when it was time for my weekly visit to the pottery. Chuey seemed surprised that I was going off to work at such a desperate time. I would never have tried to explain my real reasons for wanting to visit the potter's wheel at that time. I have never admitted my real motives to anyone, and if people had known I might have been hung as a sorceress.

I spent the brief potting session, as usual, as the all-powerful sage-king mystically ordering the whole universe. Afterwards, I hurried back to my daughter, to continue my more worldly caring for my fading child. I remember the desperate anxiety as I returned home, almost running up the lane, fearing that if she had coughed even once while I was absent, that I might be returning to a scene I could not bear to imagine.

Despite all my loving attention the child grew weaker and weaker. She became almost too weak to cough, but cough she did. I'd been trying to feed her an infusion made from willow bark, honey and milk. This seemed to sooth the terrible convulsive choking, but even administering this medicine would start an attack and in her frail condition each attack could so easily have been the last.

It was a terrible stress and it seemed almost cruel to subject her to this torture, but it also seemed our only hope and when I did get her to swallow some of the infusion it did give her some moments of peace. In that state a mere flicker of breath at the top of the throat was the only sign of life. Sometimes I felt even that had stopped and I would panic that my little one had gone. But each time she revived and I would then face the dilemma of whether to inflict more medicine on her.

In one of her moments of consciousness Chuey came in to bring more wood for the fire. The child gave him a faint smile. I looked at Chuey's gentle expression as he knelt by her. I suddenly became aware that he was not sharing in my battle.

As he lovingly stroked his daughter's cheek, I could see the acceptance on his face, and I hated him for it. I would not let my baby go. I would not allow her to die and I didn't want him infecting our protective magic space with his philosophical acceptance. I literally pushed him from the tent and held my dear little one close as I wept and vowed that I would not let even fate take my child from me.

From that moment the battle became intensely personal. I did not know what I was battling with but I wasn't going to let it take my child. Each drip of the infusion I could get her to swallow was a victory, each coughing fit survived was another step. Slowly, slowly the corner was turned. The fits decreased, allowing rest for child and mother. And slowly, slowly the crisis passed.

For weeks to come my heart would jump into my mouth each time I heard her cough, fearing that fate had been playing with us and that it had returned to claim its terrible due. But gradually the child's strength returned.

It was a great day when we dismantled the steam-tent, though it would be months before my tiny daughter was once again running and skipping around. Now, when I look at the healthy young woman she has grown into, I shudder at the thought of what might have happened if I had ever, even for one moment, allowed myself to let go of my little girl in that steamy battleground.

The children slowly returned to health but it was our marriage that was left looking sickly. The frustrations I had previously felt over Chuey's lack of ambition were almost incidental compared to what I then felt. I knew Chuey loved our children. I knew he adored our youngest. I knew he wasn't his own 'perfect man' and that he had emotions. But now I had seen that his useless philosophising extended even to his family. To me, that was something that seemed quite unforgivable.

14. LOW

One day I heard a carriage approaching and looked out to see that it was Confucius. He was alone. The house was a mess as usual. I quickly dashed around picking up the washing, which had been drying around the fire, and waited for the knock on the door. I waited, and I waited, but no knock came. Returning to the doorway I saw Confucius walking up the track in the direction of the old man's house. I knew that Confucius didn't call especially to see me, his cousin, but I expected him to at least pay me some respect. This time he had not even bothered calling in before setting off to see the old man.

I was still quietly seething at Confucius's presumptuous behaviour when the knock at the door finally came a few hours later. It was with some feeling that I opened the door, but all of my carefully rehearsed comments about him 'using our house as an inn' evaporated. My cousin was clearly very upset. All he said was "Yan," as he stepped forward and hugged me saying, "Alas, heaven is destroying me. Heaven is destroying me."

That was the start of a very sombre evening. I was impressed with the children who behaved with a marked sensitivity. Even the younger ones moderated their usual noisiness in sympathy.

Confucius never said what had happened to Yan, though he told me another story several times. He said that once, when he had been trapped in Kuang, Yan had fallen behind. When the two of them were eventually reunited Confucius had told Yan that he had thought he was dead. Yan had replied, "While you are alive Master, how would I dare to die." Yet now, Yan was gone and Confucius seemed unable to understand how he could have been so inconstant as to leave him in this way. I stayed with my cousin well into the night, trying to say all the right things, but he was inconsolable.

Early next morning there was a knock on the door. Confucius had only just risen. It was Mensa and Hussain. Confucius wearily put on his gown as they stared at him. As I brought them some tea, Hussain was asking what had happened to Yan. Again Confucius was unable to control his emotions and we were left none the wiser.

The two lads had as little success in consoling Confucius as I had managed the night before. Eventually Mensa said, with much delicate kindness, "Master, such grief is not proper."

"Well what sort of grief would be proper when mourning such a man!?" was the angry reply.

Hussain asked about the funeral arrangements. Confucius blew his nose and told them what he had planned. The lads were startled when Confucius said that he could not afford an outer coffin so a simple one would have to do.

"But master, he was your favourite student. Does he not deserve an outer coffin as well, even if it means selling your carriage?"

I was stunned by my cousin's answer, "When my own son died he had no outer coffin. Having followed in the rear of the great officers, it would not be proper that I should walk on foot." He blew his nose again.

The lads were silent, but I had to say something. "Cousin, I didn't know your son had died."

"Oh yes," he said. I was dumbfounded.

Hussain looked at Mensa for agreement and then said, "Well, I'm sure we could help out with the cost of a ..."

But Confucius interrupted his offer angrily. "Yan treated me as a father. Will you not allow me to treat him as a son?"

Hussain looked down at the floor sheepishly after his master's incomprehensible rebuke, but Confucius's comment just left me wondering whether he had ever actually treated his own son as a son. Soon after that the lads paid their respects to their master and left.

When they had gone I continued with the spinning. I didn't know what to say and I was wrapped-up in my own sad thoughts. I was fairly sure that no one in our family would be having an outer-coffin. We would be lucky to get a coffin at all, and that would only be whatever Chuey could bash together out of scraps of wood. As for his own coffin, I had already heard him discussing that with his friends. He wasn't bothered whether we even bother to bury him. He said he would be eaten by the worms if he was underground or by the birds if we just left him lying around somewhere, so why favour the worms. I reflected on the difference between my husband and my cousin and wondered whether normal people in normal households were troubled by such debates.

So that was the end of dear Yan who we had all grown extremely fond of. Now that Mensa and Hussain were studying under Confucius, it also proved to be the end of the town's little debating club.

The lads' discussions had entertained me when I first arrived in the town and on many washdays since, so I was sad to watch their final meeting at their usual table. It had been a while since I had seen all five together and much longer since I had seen them enjoying each other's company. The warmth had left the group after the king had revealed that Hans considered scholars to be one of the 'five vermin'. They had begun to take themselves very seriously and there was certainly nothing playful in the way they argued about each other's ideas that day.

As usual, they were discussing how to improve the state of the nation by taking lessons from ancient history, but there were no new sage-king stories to fuel my interest. Mensa and Hussain were generally agreeing with each other and Mo was putting forward his strange perspectives. Ian looked bored and annoyed that the same old debate was still rumbling on in its familiar circles. Hans, as always, was keeping his ideas to himself.

I watched the level of aggression rise as they argued over the rights and wrongs of various styles of government yet again. Mensa attacked everything Mo said. He did so with an air of superiority that started to sound like a child having a tantrum, expecting his opinionated speech to suddenly make everyone agree with him, then getting angry that his words were failing to have their desired effect.

They must have been having the same thoughts a few slabs up as Lily shouted out wearily, "Hey, the king was only joking! He doesn't really want any more advisors. Put a sock in it!" Her tone echoed all of our thoughts, but her uncouth plea went unheeded.

Mensa had obviously decided that Mo's input had become an unwanted nuisance. Even the angle of his body showed that he was trying to exclude Mo and his predictable interruptions. When Mo tried yet again to make a point, Mensa was scathingly dismissive saying that Mo's ideas were impractical, that they would lead to chaos and that they had no place in the real world. Mo countered that universal love would result in greater profits for everyone, at which Mensa snapped back even more viciously that they were having a serious conversation about 'real politics' and that Mo should keep his silly ideas to himself.

Mo was momentarily stunned by Mensa's aggressive outburst. He didn't say anything but then he rose from the table. I could see that he was upset as he walked away.

Ian's eyes followed him for a moment, then he scornfully echoed Mensa's words, "Real politics!"

Mensa turned on him, saying with venom that it was heretics like Mo and Ian who would stop the way of Confucius being proclaimed.

Ian stood up, scowling now with naked contempt. "The way of Confucius?" It looked as though he was about to deliver a speech on my cousin's 'way', but then decided he couldn't be bothered. "Ah!" he said, and with that he walked off across the square. Hans soon drifted off as well, leaving Mensa and Hussain with their heads together, muttering.

It was sad that the lads should end their little debating group in such an unfriendly fashion. Mensa and Hussain were still sometimes to be seen huddled together discussing their political ideas, which grew to sound more and more like my cousin's ideas. Then, even Mensa and Hussain drifted apart after arguing about whether the nature of man was essentially good or bad. They failed to agree and stopped being so close.

Mo carried on in his own sweet way, promoting his idea of universal love, his ideas getting even stranger. One time, he decided that music was a bad thing. Apparently he thought that it was to blame for the high taxes, so that became his next campaign.

The lads had grown up, as lads do, and I don't suppose there were many surprises in the directions in which they went. There was one big surprise though. Of all the participants in the loud and passionate discussions we had witnessed, the one person that nobody would have expected to succeed was Hans. You can imagine the surprise and excitement in the town when the news arrived that the king had decided to give him a job in the government after finding his book useful in dealing with troublesome scholars.

The whole town was very happy at that. Hans might not have been 'born and bred' as the other lads had been, but everyone was very proud of our adopted son. I remember thinking to myself that perhaps all of their hot air might not have gone to waste after all, and I wondered whether we would be seeing any improvements now that all of those carefully argued ideas could be put into practice.

Some interesting news emerged after the lads' final debate. It was announced that Mensa and Kim were to marry. All the fifth-day washers gave a collective knowing 'Ah, that explains it', assuming that had been the cause of the lads' bust up.

Everyone liked Kim, so we were all sad to hear that the marriage had not started well. If it hadn't been for Mensa's mother intervening, it would have been over not long after it started. Within days of the wedding Mensa had been about to throw his new wife out of the house and send her back to her parents. Apparently Mensa had come home a little earlier than expected and had entered a room to find Kim 'not sitting properly'. And that was it. That was her crime! I thought about Chuey and I and wondered whether he had *ever* seen me sitting properly.

When we all heard about it, most of the women guessed that there must have been something else going on and a few, of course, aired their lurid suspicions. But apparently not. There wasn't even a suggestion that she had been improperly dressed, let alone anything else being wrong. Mensa's sole objection to her behaviour was that Kim had not been sitting 'properly', which he judged to be unforgivably bad manners. Even her innocent smile of surprise at his dramatic over-reaction wasn't enough to make him relent, her subsequent heart-broken tears neither.

Mensa's mother was known to be a wily old battler and when Mensa told her of Kim's unacceptable sitting behaviour she turned the tables, scolding him for entering the room without announcing himself. "It is not your wife but you who are lacking manners!"

After that timely piece of mothering Mensa didn't dare to carry out his threat to cast his wife out. Kim was obviously very upset by the incident and insisted on returning to her parents anyway, but Mensa's mother persuaded Mensa to admit his fault and apologise, and with that she was able to save the marriage.

I felt for Kim. It sounded like she had a miserable introduction to married life. If things between Chuey and I had become strained, at least I could remember a happier start. But then where had it gone? Was it a happy marriage? Was I happy? In all that time I don't think I ever really considered that I was unhappy. I was annoyed, often, and sometimes angry. I was disappointed and I was certainly frustrated, but I don't think I would have admitted to being unhappy. Then came an incident which brought those feelings flooding to the surface.

Our two youngest were out the front playing, when one of them started crying. It didn't sound like anything serious, but I went outside to apply a mother's kiss and a rub to whichever part that had been bumped or bruised. After administering the kiss and a rub I noticed someone walking up the lane. They looked to be a high-ranking soldier. It is strange but as they got closer I involuntarily shouted "Sunny!" before I was even aware that I had recognised him. It was Sunny, my first love.

Sunny recognised me instantly. We stood looking at each other, both of us knowing that even though nothing was being said, there were many things that were not being said. I think it was Sunny who eventually broke the silence, making some polite compliment about our little house and about the two muddy children at my feet.

I responded, politely complimenting him on his smart uniform.

The only piece of real communication between us was when he said, "Yes, I heard you, er...," and waved a finger to indicate the house and the children, and all that they implied.

"Yes," I admitted, even though it hadn't been an accusation. I remembered to thank him for the rice.

"And how many, er?" he said, looking at the children.

"Five," I said weakly.

Sunny nodded and smiled as a congratulation.

I felt very dowdy. I didn't ask him all of the questions I was so desperate to ask. 'Did he ever marry? Did he ever regret, or wonder what might have been? Did he ever think of me? Did he think that we might yet ever ...'

The little politenesses dried-up.

"Sorry, I didn't know you lived here." Sunny pointed up the track. "I was just on my way to visit the old man, actually," he added, almost as an excuse.

I think it was me who said, "Well, it's been nice to see you again."

He looked at me intently, nodding. "It's good to see that," he paused, "that you're so settled."

And that was it. He walked up the track and I went inside and wept and wept. A while later I came out and looked up the valley, but Sunny was already out of view. Even with all the emotion of seeing him again, I remember wondering for a moment why an immaculately dressed military man might be striding up a muddy track to see an uncommunicative old man.

After Sunny had passed by the front door I would have admitted I was unhappy. I couldn't have denied it. In those sad times hardly a day went past that I didn't embarrass myself with some tears. Most of the time I didn't even know why I was crying. What effect those tears had on the children, or on Chuey, I do not know.

I felt as if I was trapped, though it would be hard to say exactly what I was trapped in. The children were growing up and all my hopes for them, and for myself, seemed to be certain to come to nothing. It seemed we would never be able to provide for them in a manner which anyone would consider adequate. It made matters worse that I was tied to a man who had no interest in even trying to do so. Instead, he was more interested in whether starlight received an answer from nothingness or not. It seemed that the children would be condemned to suffer the same struggles we endured.

That was my lowest, weakest point.

My state of mind improved once I started taking matters into my own hands. The first occasion that I remember was when a scholar knocked on our door the day before market day. By then I had stopped even trying to be polite to the visitors. I pointedly told Chuey, in front of the guest, that he would need to empty the fish-traps in time for the following day's market, but he just made some excuse why it wouldn't be a good time to check the traps. I was livid and said I would go and check them anyway, myself. That was a bold move as I hadn't been directly involved with any of the fishing activities before. Chuey seemed relaxed about that and tried to describe where he had left them.

Chuey had shown me the fish-traps once many years before when we were first married, but I had never checked or emptied one. Chuey had probably been right in saying it hadn't been a good time to check them, but I did manage to retrieve three small fish that at least provided a meal for our family that night even if there was nothing to take to market. That little step marked a change. Before then I would passively fume with frustration at our family's poverty. Afterwards, I found I had a way to get out and do something about it.

Chuey was happy to go along with the shift in our roles. As I began to spend more time fishing, he took on more of the cooking and domestic duties. I knew that Chuey generally fished in the smaller river. He had once told me that there's less water there so it's easier to find the fish. Over time he showed me his favourite spots and showed me how to tie all the knots I would need. As my fishing became a regular part of our routine, he went on to explain when he used a line and when nets worked best, pointing out the places where it was safe to use a net and where the riverbed was too rough. I had spent long enough mending the nets to know the importance of such information and paid careful attention to the lessons. He also showed me the balm he used to keep his skin from cracking when fishing with nets all day. He even tried to show me his technique for spearing turtles.

There are many steps to learn before you can get a fish on the bank. I learned those skills quickly. I would head off to the river excited, determined and keen to succeed, but in those early days I would often return with only meagre portions for dinner. Then, gradually, my fishing got better. It is hard to describe that change. It was subtle but a little like my experiences at the potter's wheel. It wasn't that I suddenly became the 'sage-king of the river bank', but there was something of that. There was less frantic trying, and more quiet focus. Less doing, more calm. Calmness helped my fishing and the fishing helped me to be calm. I might not have quite reached the 'non-fishing of the true artist', but I found I was taking home more fish and better fish, and it felt good. Returning from a day at the river with a fine catch, I even slipped into Chuey's habit of giving fish away. The potter often benefitted.

As my fishing improved, the family's diet improved, but we were still pitifully poor. Even though I loved the fishing, I still held on to my resentment at having to do it. My frustration at Chuey and his endless stream of visitors continued. If I got home and Chuey decided to carry on philosophising rather than help me clean the catch, or if he had been too busy discussing the Tao to get the evening meal prepared, my anger would quickly return.

*Who can (make) the muddy water (clear)? Let it
be still, and it will gradually become clear.*

TAO TE CHING CHAPTER 15

15. A STRANGE PERSPECTIVE

Late one afternoon, while I was preparing my tackle for the next day's fishing, a carriage drew up outside our house. A smartly dressed older man stepped down. His manner was quite different to any of Chuey's usual sort of visitors and, from the way he politely asked if Chuey was at home, I guessed that he had not come to chat about the Tao. I called out to Chuey without interrupting my work.

Chuey came out. He didn't seem to know the man and I could tell that this was no casual conversation, so I watched carefully as I continued to slowly wind line onto a spool. The man seemed to ask Chuey a question. Chuey appeared undecided, looking at the ground and shaking his head. Then it looked as though Chuey asked a question. After a short pause he got an answer then, with some reluctance it seemed, Chuey started to nod his head.

Chuey walked over to me. He told me that the prince had asked him to go and have a chat with someone. Then he said, "You'll be alright for a few days?" It had been somewhere between a question and a reassuring statement, but there was a weight in his words. He added, "I'll try to make sure you get to know if, if it's, er, going to be longer than that." He looked me directly in the eye, gave a little smile and a nod, then walked to the carriage, climbed up and they drove off. When I went inside I found that Chuey hadn't even made a start on making the dinner yet. I picked up the knife and chopping board, muttering under my breath.

The children were more independent by then and could mostly look after themselves. Even if Chuey had gone off to tell one of the prince's friends about starlight and nothingness, it didn't seem to make much difference to us, so the next morning I headed off to the river as planned. On the way my head was full of black thoughts about it not really mattering if Chuey ever came back.

There had been plenty of rain in the week before and the river was still high. I knew that the fast flowing water would make some of the stretches unfishable, so instead I headed to a bend where the water is always deep and slow. Arriving at the river, my mood calmed as the quest for fish took over from the resentment at my husband's sudden holiday. I walked along the bank looking for a good place to fish, but ended up in one of my usual spots where there is just enough marginal weed and trees overhead.

It was a soft grey day with no wind at all. By the time I was setting up my rod a gentle drizzle had started to fall. This was a place for line fishing, which was always my favourite method, just like Cousin Confucius. Baiting the hook, I looked at the smooth surface of the river and felt a tingle of anticipation.

When fishing with a line and float, that tip of a duck-feather quill becomes your only link to another world, the world of fish. Flicking the float out onto the dark water, I was in contact with that world. I didn't have to wait long until the float disappeared and I caught a small bream, then another. It was beginning to look as though I would be taking home a good catch.

I rebaited the hook and cast the line. The float righted itself. The stillness of the day underlined every movement. The tip of the float was my only focus as it moved slowly down with the river's flow. The tip bobbed slightly, it paused and then slid under the water. I pulled the rod up sharply, which by then had become a well-ingrained reflex. In response there was unyielding resistance. For the briefest of moments I suspected the hook was snagged on something, but then I felt the rod move with the unmistakable feel of life at the other end of the line, the satisfying pull of a substantial fish.

When I had started fishing, this was the time I would lose most fish. Judging when to give line to the fish and when to take it back is an art that I had learned through many disappointments. The fish was certainly large and strong. It pulled hard and I had to let it swim out, but then I needed to slow it, and hold it. The rod arched dangerously, the line stretched taught, but it held, and slowly, with great effort, I turned the fish back. Once more the fish pulled away from me, but again I slowed it and turned it. The line started cutting through the water rapidly towards a patch of lilies to the right. I held my breath. Heaving with as much force as I dared, I managed to steer it away from the lilies, back towards the open water, and I could breathe again. After a few more dives, the fish was tiring and I was able to pull it, slowly slowly upwards. First, the float came into view. Peering into the water, I could see a large golden shape beneath. When the fish came to the surface I gasped at its size. Keeping the rod well bent, I kept its head up as I pulled the fish over the marginal weeds, towards the bank. It was a huge carp, very saleable.

Once the fish was on the mud, I removed the hook from its enormous mouth, panting at the thrill of such a catch. I bent down to try to lift it, but its great weight made it hard. Eventually, managing to get my arms under it, I hugged the fish tightly and made a step towards the top of the bank, keen to get my prize to safety. As I struggled to get a firm foothold up the slippery mud, the fish suddenly writhed. I tried to readjust my hold but the fish moved again and, with its great weight, it slipped out of my arms. One bounce off the muddy bank and a flap took it to the water's edge. Another flap moved it further into the water where it lay half submerged in the weeds. Both the fish and I froze for a moment before I frantically slipped down the bank and dived to grab the fish, but with a wave of its thick tail and a twist it had disappeared and I was left grasping only weed. I desperately felt around, but the fish was gone.

I screamed in frustration. I slapped both hands down onto the water and screamed, and I slapped and I screamed, and slapped and screamed, and I screamed. I screamed at the fish, I screamed at Chuey, but mostly I screamed at myself, for my haste and for not securing the fish properly. I screamed at EVERYTHING!!! Then, still kneeling in the cold muddy water, I cried. I had let a fish slip through my fingers that I could have traded for enough rice to feed the family for a month.

When I arrived home, our youngest came out to meet me. She always asked 'what are we having for dinner tonight?' Before she could speak I snapped "Don't ask!" She started crying, saying she wanted daddy to come home.

The next day was washday. I wasn't very interested in the women's conversation that morning. New regulars had started coming on the fifth day. They were younger and I found their chattering irritating. I wasn't paying attention to their gossip. Instead, my mind was still going over each and every detail of the previous day's crushing loss of the carp, cursing myself as I thought of all the ways I could have avoided the calamity.

I paid more attention to the conversation around me when one of the new women mentioned Confucius. In a reverential tone she said that she had heard that he had gained miraculous strength and that he was the only person who could lift the heavy wooden bar that locked the great gates in the city wall. Lily told them that I was his cousin and they looked at me with surprise and respect. I nodded and carried on with my washing.

One of the women asked me, "Is it true that a unicorn appeared at his birth and spat out a piece of jade with a prophecy written on it, saying that he would become an uncrowned emperor?"

I told them that my aunty hadn't mentioned anything like that happening. They ignored my dour comment, another of the new women saying, "And you know, it was Confucius who went up to the robbers' camp to fight that evil Robber Chih." That was enough for me. I picked up my washing and walked off shaking my head.

Even as I got busier with the fishing, I was still making time for my weekly climb to see the old man in the upper valley. It always helped my mood. Just like the ancestor shrine, his house seemed to have a peace about it. No matter what my state of mind as I climbed up the rocky slope to his hut, it was always lighter as I descended. Still torturing myself for my lapses in losing the carp, and annoyed by the conversation at the washing slabs, I set off up the lane with a few rice cakes.

As usual, I announced my arrival in a cheery fashion, entering to find him sitting in exactly the same position he had been the previous week. And, as usual, my greeting was met with not a hint of acknowledgement, no movement, not even a blink, but I had got used to that. It had become a very comfortable habit.

I started by telling him how I had lost a big fish the day before. I flashed around with the broom as I told him that Chuey was away, then I said how annoying I had found the conversation at the slabs that morning. All the while the old man sat there motionless and, as usual, never giving the slightest hint that he found any of this information at all interesting. Despite our strange relationship, I had grown very fond of the old man, looking upon him as something of a substitute grandfather, though for all I knew he was more like a great-grandfather or even a great-great grandfather.

I opened the door to sweep out the dust and a chill mountain breeze blew in. Autumn was already well advanced and I suddenly had the idea that it might be unwise for the old man to stay up in the hills over winter. I closed the door and shivered. I asked the old man whether he had any relatives he could spend the winter with. There was no answer, of course, but I saw this as an important question. I walked closer to him, looked into his face and said very clearly, as though he might be dim-witted or hard of hearing, "We haven't got a lot of room, but if you want to, I don't think Chuey would mind, that is if you don't mind being a bit squashed-up,..."

There was no change to his features to show gratitude or resentment at the offer, or anything else for that matter. There was no clue in his face whatsoever, so I tried again to coax an answer. "Wouldn't you like to be down, around with people, just for the winter? You could come back here, to your house, when the weather improves. It would certainly be more," I paused, looking around his bare shack, "more lively."

I stared into his face. There wasn't even a flicker of movement to answer my intense questioning. But then he started to speak. He spoke as I had never heard him speak before, sounding as though he was indeed the Yellow Emperor.

"The multitude of men look satisfied and pleased, as if enjoying a full banquet, as if mounted on a tower in spring. I alone seem listless and still, my desires having as yet given no indication of their presence. I am like an infant which has not yet smiled. I look dejected and forlorn, as if I had no home to go to.

The multitude of men all have enough and to spare. I alone seem to have lost everything. My mind is that of a stupid man; I am in a state of chaos." His words of self-deprecation were wholly at odds with his delivery. He seemed to have grown, and was he glowing? I could even imagine that he levitated slightly as he spoke.

I was about to try to reassure him that I didn't think he was stupid, but he was already continuing, not sounding as though he needed any sort of reassurance. "Ordinary men look bright and intelligent, while I alone seem to be benighted. They look full of discrimination, while I alone am dull and confused. I seem to be carried about as on the sea, drifting as if I had nowhere to rest. All men have their spheres of action, while I alone seem dull and incapable, like a rude borderer."

He seemed to almost smile. "But wherein I most differ from other men is that I value the nursing mother." With that, the old man stopped and was once again silent and motionless.

I wondered to myself whether that had been an answer to my question, but aloud I repeated, "The nursing mother", nodding my head, even though I hadn't really known what he had meant.

He turned his head slowly to look at me and said, "The Tao." His head turned back to face forward and he was once more still.

The old man had become my honorary ancestor, a hazy link to my family and to all that I had left behind in my home village. The time I spent with him had become my own ceremony of filial piety, my own ritual offering. With one word, that all changed. As I left the old man's cottage that day I looked back at him and saw just a wizened old man.

As I left the old man's cottage and started back down the track to our house, the wind had got colder. The tears which rolled down my cheeks were a little saltier and perhaps a little more bitter. Then even the tears stopped. And as I made my way down the rocky path I compared myself to the child who had first moved to this town and who had fallen in love with Chuey on something of a whim. In that moment I certainly felt very grown-up: the blackest, emptiest, loneliest, most grown-up feeling anyone could possibly imagine suffering.

Chuey still hadn't returned by the time I was next due at the pottery. I had been disappointed that the children had not behaved better in his absence. I would return from the river to find them bickering, with no start made on preparing dinner and without the show of respect that I felt my day's labour deserved. That morning I told the children what chores I expected each of them to have completed by the time I returned. As I left, the mood in the house was not good and I was glad to leave.

The potter was always pleased to see me. He was a good friend. Not that we spoke much. Maybe that is why we had continued to get along so well. We talked about clay, about firing and we talked about pots, and that was about all we talked about, but it was always a pleasant exchange.

He mentioned that the trader had recently asked if we had any of our more exotic pieces available. As I reached for my apron, he said merrily, "So, if the clay is 'flowing', don't bother with the usual stock, just go with the er ..." He paused.

"Just go with the what?" I asked flatly, suspecting he meant 'with the Tao'. He must have sensed my unspoken resentment as he just shrugged, gave a little smile of appeasement and left me alone to put my apron on.

I sat down at the wheel. Usually this was the time that my mind would clear and I would feel the peace of my sanctuary as I slipped into my sage-king fantasy role, but this time my anger at the wording of the potter's comment still filled my head. It seemed as though everyone and everything was against me. My mind did not clear.

I went through the now reflex actions of preparing the clay, slapping it onto the turntable and starting the wheel turning. My leg pushed movement into the stone disc but I had not yet become the sage-king with the perfectly empty head. I was still me. I was still very much 'myself'. I thought of the potter's near-mention of the Tao and of his weak smile when he sensed my annoyance, which annoyed me even more.

The wheel gained speed and the clay juddered and shook as it momentarily resisted the force of my hands. Centring the clay had by then become second nature, but that day I paused. Maybe I was waiting to compose myself before taking the clay to that special place of stillness, aware that I still hadn't shed the cares of the outside world. But the peace did not come. My mind was still angry at the potter's desertion, joining the old man and everyone else. The potter really was the last friend. I felt completely alone.

After feeling the clay's violent, living motion for a moment, I found myself digging my elbows into my sides and the rebellious movement ceased. I watched the clay spinning true and steady in my hands while my leg automatically pulsed more and more speed into the wheel.

Almost as if in a dream, I watched my hands as they started to use the magic point of stillness and the whirling motion of the wheel to begin working the clay, but my mind was elsewhere. It had moved on from the potter to the old man's mention of the Tao at the end of his strange speech. I thought back to his nobly stated words about appearing to be unintelligent. What was all that about? "*All men have their spheres of action, while I alone seem dull and incapable, like a rude borderer.*"

As I stared at my fingers forming the clay into a workable shape I could hear the old man's words as clearly as if he had been sitting there at my side. "*My mind is that of a stupid man; I am in a state of chaos.*"

I looked on passively as my fingers gently rested on the centre of the clay and saw the hollow magically begin to form. I watched my hands and the slowly transforming clay. It was like being back in that first visit to the pottery, watching the potter's exhibition of his talents. They hardly seemed to be my hands at all. I wasn't the sage-king, but my sage-king was making a pot for me while I watched. And all the while the old man's words filled my head. "*Ordinary men look bright and intelligent, while I alone seem to be benighted. They look full of discrimination, while I alone am dull and confused.*"

I remembered Lily telling us that the old man was the Yellow Emperor, first of the sage-kings. The link between the sound of his voice in my head and sage-king's actions occurring before my eyes struck me as funny, but it was a hollow, distant humour. With a morbid fascination I stared at my hands as they automatically performed their miracle of creation, beginning to draw-up the sides of the pot. I thought of my visits to the old man, with him sitting there, motionless, his back straight and his gaze clear, while I chattered on.

It was as though I was in a trance. I tried to concentrate on the task of making the pot but my efforts met with no success. This was a daydream I could not awaken from. I was there but somehow not there, present but somehow unneeded. I tried to block out the old man's words, to return to the simple silent peace of being the sage-king who was making the pot, but the more I tried the louder the words became. "*I alone seem to be benighted*," echoed his assured, passive tones.

I watched my hands in their steady work. My eyes stayed fixed upon them as they slowly formed the pot, but my attention wandered. I became aware of the turntable as if for the first time. With fascination I remembered that it was just the top of an up-turned log. My mind followed the log down to the stone wheel spinning below. It almost made me laugh as I sensed my leg kicking motion into the great mass. I had forgotten my leg, and when I noticed its constant pulsing motion it felt like someone else's leg. Again that seemed funny, like a joke in an unbelievable dream. Then the smile disappeared as I suddenly thought of all the rushing momentum of the wheel, with the stone's rough edge racing round at great speed. It seemed almost impossible that the pot could survive in the middle of that frantic energy. It was a shock. As the sage-king I had never considered what was happening down there, being fully absorbed in the stillness of the clay world and the growing pot. Thinking of all of that whirling motion below, made me feel dizzy.

But my hands were still. With some apprehension I watched as they started to draw the sides of the pot higher and thinner.

And still the old man's words were clear and insistent. "*The multitude look satisfied and pleased; as if enjoying a full banquet. I alone seem listless and still.*" I certainly felt listless and still as I watched my hands performing their delicate operation. For some reason the idea of the 'satisfied multitude' brought Lily back to mind, with her raucous laugh and robust sense of humour. And I thought of all of the other fifth-day morning washers, and of Sue and her new house. I felt that thought as a little jolt which was echoed when I compared it to our own little house. Those jolts felt like shudders in uncentred clay. As I looked at my hands, delicately drawing the pot into something elegant and fragile, and as I remembered the fearful destructive force raging somewhere below, it seemed inevitable that any such movement would bring instant catastrophe.

Thoughts of our crowded little house led to thoughts of the children, and those led to thoughts of growing up with my own brothers and sisters and thoughts of our village. Each image was felt as a jerk and a judder, pulling or pushing me one way or the other. The height, the speed and the whirr of the images made me feel sick with fear. It seemed to be just a matter of time before everything would shake itself to pieces. I knew, even from my first potting experience, how suddenly disaster can strike with the wheel spinning at that speed. When the clay is even slightly off-centre the pot will eventually tear itself apart, but what happens if the potter is slightly off-centre as she tries to rule the clay-world?

As I watched the images whirl around, each twitch seemed certain to topple the tower of clay. But it didn't. The clay stayed quite still between my fingers, the sides of the pot growing beautifully under the sage-king's passive control. I drank in that peace and steadied my nerves. Remembering my village brought other memories. I remembered our courtship and Chuey's proposal. I thought of Chuey, and of Sunny. I felt the pull of them both, and it was almost as though they were chasing each other round the edge of the wheel which wobbled, juddered and shuddered with their weight. Panic brought my attention back to the pot, but the stillness had survived. I steadied my nerves and dared to look again.

I saw myself, moving in directions which were constantly thwarted by the spinning of the wheel. There was Leah and her husband. There was also a prime minister's wife taking tea with Leah, now dressed as an elegant courtier. And there was the dusty potter and Mad Joe, and Confucius, Robber Chih and the king. Everything in my world spun round frantically, jerking me one way and then the other, each movement threatening to bring the whole world crashing down.

But in my hands was stillness, my fingers delicately following the graceful, growing shape. A half-smile of relief came when I realised that the stillness remained, there in the clay between my fingers, regardless. Even in my dizziness and vertigo, the stillness was unaffected. It was a stillness I could return to at will, but more, it was one I never really left. It wasn't something I needed to cling to, it was in my hands the whole time. Relief grew into a sense of peace.

Surer of that place of stillness I took time to look at the whirling images, but now without the fear. I could feel the pulls and the pushes as they raced around the rim of the wheel, feeling why each one jolted my world with feelings of 'good' and 'bad' pulling and pushing in different directions as the wheel raced around. I could see all of that and I could feel all of that, but at the same time I could be at the centre, where there was stillness. Even in the midst of all that frightening whir of motion, I could be calm, my hands showing the way with their serene control over the clay world.

It is hard to describe that feeling, looking at my life from the peaceful centre. It might sound cold and detached, but it was quite the opposite. I could clearly see and feel my attachments to all of the things in my life. The calmness came from a place that just happened to be at the centre of the wheel, the eye of the storm, but the centre was not separate from the wheel, the centre was at peace with all its attachments.

I certainly wasn't detached as I beheld my life rushing round the potter's wheel. Tears came into my eyes as I realised just how much I loved everything in my life. The feeling was both surprising and overwhelming. It took my breath away. I watched everything rushing around madly and I felt for it all, but with a peace and an acceptance which no words could ever adequately describe. As I watched my chaotic world from the stillness of the pot growing in my hands, I realised that all of the pulling and pushing came from me, it came from the sage-king.

I watched myself in my childhood and I saw all my ancestors stretching back in time, back beyond memory and back beyond any written history. And there were our children, each so different, then the children's children's children, with me long gone, and with my children long gone. I could see Chuey and Hue, useless and useful, whirling round the wheel. And there was Chuey and I, together, with the space he gives me. I saw all of that, and I was at peace with it all. From the centre of the wheel, I was at peace with it all and I loved it all. I loved it all so much! And in the still clarity of that moment I was aware that my love of everything was being returned, by everything, and I could feel that love surrounding me.

I left the circling images and was once more at the centre, back to the elegant pot which my sage-king was causing to grow. I went there, not because I needed to, or even because I wanted to, but just because it was peaceful there.

I watched my fingers caressing the stillness of the growing pot and I was the sage-king again. I slipped easily back into my old fantasy, with the sage-king's power filling the clay world, and then back into 'being' the clay world. I was the pot growing in the centre of the wheel but, with a smile on my lips, I could now see how everything was part of that growth: the turntable, the log, the disc of stone, my leg pushing it, and everything around me.

It sounds strange now, but in that moment it seemed to me that I was a child growing in the womb of everything, right in the peaceful centre of all the swirling motion of everything. This was much more than a daydream. For a moment, in that still, safe place, I really felt I was that unborn child. The feeling brought with it more tears which rolled down my cheeks. The tears rolled and rolled. Not tears of sadness nor tears of happiness. Not tears of relief or regret either. But they rolled and rolled.

As the tears rolled, while I held the pot in my hands, I heard the words of the old man. "*But wherein I most differ from other men is that I value the nursing mother.*"

Slowly I turned the two ideas over in my mind, the child in the womb and the child at the mother's breast. As I compared the old man's nursing mother with the womb I had found myself in, I recognised in his words a poetry which described my dream-like feeling. I thought of the love I was feeling in my mother's womb and of his valuing of his own nursing mother and I could see they were the same.

Lost in thought, I took my hands from the partly-made pot. My leg stopped its pulsing, allowing the wheel to spin quietly by itself. The tears had stopped.

I wiped my eyes with my palms – yes, my filthy, clayed-up palms, then realising that I had just wiped the mess all over my face, I tried wiping it off with the apron, which probably made it look even worse, but my mind wasn't on my appearance. I hung the apron back on the hook. My breath was coming in fits and starts as I opened the door.

Outside the world looked the same. It had not been shaken to pieces by spinning around so madly upon the potter's wheel. I started walking up the lane, past our house, up the track and on, up towards the old man's house.

16. MORE PERSPECTIVE, MAYBE

Walking up from the ridge into the old man's valley, I was still desperately trying to gather my thoughts before arriving at his door. Suddenly it was too late. The old man was sitting outside. Every other time I had visited he had been in the same spot inside his house, but that day he was sitting out in the midday sunshine. As I approached I could see that he had washed his hair and was spreading it very slowly and deliberately over his shoulders to dry.

I stopped a few paces from him and began searching for whatever it was I had come to say. I searched for words to ask him something about 'wherein he most differs from most men' now that I had seen some of that difference in myself. I tried to form a question, but as I stood there none of the words I started to say were up to the task. All were swallowed before escaping.

The old man hadn't acknowledged my arrival, but then he did look up at me. He silently raised his hand to stop whatever words I was preparing to force out. With my dumb struggling ended, I stood and watched as he returned to arranging his hair. When each strand had been carefully placed he looked at me again and then began to speak.

He spoke quietly, slowly, deliberately. "There is a man in a nearby town. He makes his living in the market there as a diviner, using straws, cards or whatever other methods his customers prefer. He admits that this is a lowly occupation but he pursues it because he feels that by practising it he can benefit the common people. When people come to him with questions about something which is evil or improper he uses the oracle as an excuse to advise them on what he feels is right, using whatever the circumstances may be to lead the people to the right course of action. Over half of the people follow his advice. He spends his days instructing the people in the dictates of conventional morality in this fashion, but when he has made enough money for the day he shuts up his stall, lowers the blinds and then gives instruction to certain pupils on the Way which is beyond right and wrong, the Tao. In the evening, when the pupils have all gone and he is alone, he returns to that which is beyond names, even beyond the name of 'Tao'. This is the same man teaching in the mornings and in the afternoons, and he is the same man during the evening, and also when he goes to sleep at night."

And that was it! The old man's gaze was back on the infinite distance. I bowed, a little uncertainly, not sure that I had really received that which I had come for, but realising the old man had finished delivering that which he had to impart. His head dipped almost imperceptibly to acknowledge my acknowledgement, bringing the lesson to a close.

I left the old man drying his hair in the sun and started to make my way down the path home, laughing to myself. On the way I picked some herbs for dinner. When I arrived back I went inside to put the herbs on the chopping board ready for preparing dinner later. Our youngest saw me and instantly started to laugh. Then I remembered the dried clay slurry still smeared all over my face. I picked her up and we laughed together. After washing my face I went back to the pottery to clear up the mess I had left.

The potter seemed concerned and asked if anything was wrong. He told me that he had finished the pot. It hadn't been a great success, but that it would do for the local market. He had also cleaned up for me. We shared an embarrassed smile. I didn't bother trying to explain what had happened but thanked him, apologised and said it wouldn't happen again.

After my funny turn at the potter's wheel I was desperate for Chuey to return. My mind went back to the way he had looked at me before he had left, and to his deliberate and carefully chosen words. Where had the prince asked him to go? As the days passed my fears grew, but then one day I heard one of the children shout, "Dad's back!"

I ran out and there was Chuey walking up the lane. He looked just as he did when he had driven off in the carriage, except I noticed that, strangely, he was now wearing a pair of felt boots, the sort I had seen the king's fencers wearing whenever they had stopped in town. We all ran to meet him and I hugged him tightly, very glad to have him back. He was clearly very happy to be home.

Later, I got rather emotional as I tried to apologise for the way I had been behaving. Chuey used his thumb to wipe a tear from my cheek and gallantly understated it all, saying, "Yes, I noticed your pool got a little murky for a while." He didn't hide his happiness at the change in me. He said, "Welcome back." And how true it was. I don't know where I had been but it did seem that I had come back home. It was as though I suddenly rediscovered everything that was sweet and beautiful in my life, and it is only with effort now that I can remember why I had ever 'left'.

17. YET MORE PERSPECTIVE

L ife quickly returned to normal after Chuey's return. I was still fishing and potting, doing my weekly washing and going up to see the old man. The routine was the same but it all felt so very different. Something of my potting-wheel revelation remained. Other people noticed the change in me and the general opinion at the washing slabs was that I had taken a lover. My protests of innocence were ignored as they discussed who the lucky man might be.

Then one day, returning from a day's fishing, I saw that there was another fine carriage with a coachman waiting outside our house. I anxiously wondered what it might mean this time, but as I approached the house I heard laughter. Looking in, I gasped when I saw that Chuey was sitting with the prince. Chuey noticed me and beckoned me in, but I excused myself saying I needed to clean up.

After scrubbing my hands and trying to wipe the worst of the fishiness from my trousers, I went inside wondering whether I should bow. Chuey and the royal visitor were sitting by the fire and they were still laughing so bowing didn't seem necessary. They already had a cup of tea each so I poured one for myself. I was about to take my tea outside but the prince called to me in a friendly tone, "Well, what do you think of your husband's performance then?"

I didn't know what to say. "Sorry, what performance?"

The prince looked surprised, then looked quite serious. He turned to Chuey and said, "What? You haven't told your wife what happened?" He then turned to me with a smile on his face and said, "My dear lady, please join us. I think you ought to hear what your husband has been up to."

The prince cast a sideways glance at Chuey, who looked bashful. The prince was clearly enjoying the chance to relate the details of Chuey's recent trip.

Apparently the prince had sent one of the officers with a request to Chuey that day after the ministers had met in secret to discuss what to do about the king's love of fencing. It was felt that the king had gone mad or that he'd been taken over by an evil spirit, such was his single-minded passion and his ever worsening temper. His interest in swordsmen had grown to such a level that providing for his entertainment had become a huge drain on the kingdom's resources, with him maintaining over 3000 swordsmen at the palace merely for the pleasure of seeing them fight. It was reported that neighbouring countries had already begun preparations to take advantage of our weakened state. Not only had the king's obsession with fencing caused him to neglect his royal duties but it had cost the lives of several loyal ministers, executed for merely daring to raise the problem with the king. Understandably, no one wanted to be the next to try. The prince looked rather awkward as he admitted that he had asked Chuey to come to the capital, feeling that it was his last hope of making his father reconsider his expensive pastime.

Chuey told the prince that he had heard that the king would see no one but fencers so requested a full swordsman's outfit complete with a loose cap held on with simple rough straps, robes cut short behind and felt boots. After three days Chuey's outfit was ready and, dressed as a fencer, Chuey went to the palace.

On hearing of Chuey's arrival, the king apparently drew his sword and sat waiting for him. The prince described with admiration how Chuey did not quicken his step as he approached the throne and, when in front of the king, he didn't even bow his head.

"Why has the prince brought you before me?" demanded the king.

"I have heard that the King delights in swords, so I have come to show you mine."

"Oh yes, and what sort of fight can you put up with that sword of yours?" asked the king, unimpressed.

"My sword can kill one person every ten paces and after a thousand miles it will still not be faltering."

"Ha! There can be no one else like you under Heaven!" laughed the king sceptically, but impressed by Chuey's audacious manner and his bold claims.

As the prince related this, I gave Chuey a disbelieving look. He seemed slightly uncomfortable listening to the prince's account, but he didn't dispute any of it.

The prince continued saying that the king then beckoned to one of the ministers. After the king had said a few words in his ear, the minister hurried away. The king looked Chuey up and down slowly. The prince said that he stepped forward and tried to speak to his father, but the king held up his hand to stop him.

The king sat in silence until the minister returned. He was now accompanied by a swordsman. He wasn't especially tall but thickset, with tousled-hair and a spiky beard. I had seen such men in our town on their way to the palace, looking about fiercely and living up to their reputation for talking only about their aggressive sport.

"So, you're a fighter, you say," the king said to Chuey with gleeful menace. "Well", he paused for dramatic effect, "let's see what you can do."

The prince said that he urgently stepped forward and again tried to speak. He stressed that he had only ever intended Chuey to talk to the king.

The king held up his hand again with a stern look to end the prince's interference. Then, to Chuey and the swordsman, he said gently, "Well, fight then."

I looked at Chuey, aghast. I knew he was good with a sword, but the king's fencers were a breed apart.

The prince described how the swordsman bowed to the king, drew his sword and started to circle Chuey. Chuey drew his own sword and moved round. Neither man made any move for a while, just circling each other. Suddenly the swordsman attacked with a rapid sequence of strokes. With awkward reactions, Chuey just about managed to fend off the lethal cutting and stabbing movements. The two men returned to circling each other once more.

The swordsman nodded, perhaps to acknowledge Chuey's skills in surviving his first attack or, more likely, confident that the fight would soon be ending in his favour.

The swordsman's next attack seemed to catch Chuey by surprise. Only two instinctive flinches with his own sword kept the swordsman's blade from chopping into him.

The prince looked at me shaking his head, anxious to let me know that yet again he tried to halt the fight. He said he had shouted "Your Majesty!" and again stepped forward. The king had simply glowered at him. The prince said, rather apologetically, that he knew then that he was powerless to help Chuey.

After the prince's interruption, the swordsman started to grin. He circled one way, then the other way, and back again. He made little feints left and right, toying with Chuey.

The prince apologised that he couldn't fully explain what occurred next as it all happened in a single movement, so fast it was a blur. It started when the swordsman lunged at Chuey with a gleeful shout, swinging his sword high. After first appearing to back away, Chuey instead thrust his body forward, inside the arc of the swordsman's blade. They crashed chest to chest, Chuey's non-sword-arm elbow going high over his foe's sword-arm and his free hand gripping the man's upper arm. In the same motion Chuey's right heel hooked up his opponent's left foot before Chuey stepped back, dragging the swordsman's leg with him. As Chuey moved back he brought his elbow down hard, trapping the man's sword-arm and forcing his unbalanced foe down onto one knee. The instant of motion ended in sudden stillness with Chuey standing over his kneeling opponent. The two men's faces were almost touching as Chuey held his sword high, its tip touching the man's neck, ready to thrust down into his chest.

It took a moment for the disbelieving swordsman to recover from the shock of the situation he suddenly found himself in. With a grunt, he tried to free his sword-arm, but Chuey forced his elbow down harder to maintain his lock on the man's arm. Chuey emphasised his dominance by pressing the tip of his sword slightly more firmly against his foe's neck, starting a tiny trickle of blood. Heeding the warning, the swordsman ceased his struggle and awaited his fate.

The prince described how the frowning king gave a slight gesture with his hand, his fingers slicing through the air, instructing Chuey to end his opponent's life. Instead, Chuey shoved the swordsman away. The man sprawled onto the floor, touching the tiny cut on his neck and examining the blood on his fingers.

"No. He can serve you in better ways than that Your Majesty," said Chuey defiantly.

The king was at once startled, livid and fascinated. The prince, with wide-eyed admiration, explained that no one ever dared to disobey the king, particularly on matters of sword fighting.

The king stared at Chuey. Moments passed. Eventually, the king started nodding slowly and muttered, almost as a whisper, "I will see this man fight again." Aloud, he ordered, "Prepare my fighters," then thundered, "All of them!"

The prince said that the king was enraged at Chuey's impudence, but elated to have such a challenge to his much-prized fighters. He proceeded to have all of his fencers fight duels with each other for seven days to determine which six would have the honour of facing Chuey in combat. The prince added that over sixty of the fighters were killed or injured during those bouts.

On the appointed day of the contest, the top six fighters and Chuey were commanded to appear before the king in the great hall. When the fighters and courtiers were assembled, the king asked Chuey, "Which choice of arms do you favour, the long sword or the short?"

"I am prepared to use any type, but I have three swords in mind, any of which could serve Your Majesty. Allow me to tell you of the three, then you yourself may choose." Apparently the king was keen on Chuey's suggestion and sat up, leaning forward on his throne, to hear of the three swords.

"The three swords are, the sword of the Son of Heaven, the sword of a Prince of a State and the sword of the common man. Would it please Your Majesty to hear of the Sword of the Son of Heaven first?"

"It would," said the king eagerly.

"The sword of the Son of Heaven covers everything within the four frontiers, extending even as far as the neighbouring barbarians, and reigning from the western mountains to the eastern sea. Following the course of yin and yang and the five elements, of the laws of justice and clemency, it stand alert in spring and summer. It is rampant in autumn and winter. Nothing can resist this blade when taken from its sheath and brandished. Raised high, it cleaves the firmaments. Swung low it severs the very veins of the earth. It forces everyone into submission. That is the sword of the Son of Heaven."

The king didn't speak and Chuey carried on. "Now let me tell you about the sword of a prince of a state. It is a weapon made of bravery, fidelity, courage, loyalty and wisdom. It is brandished over a principality, conforming to the laws of heaven and earth and the time. Raised high, there is nothing above it. Swung low, there is nothing below it. This blade maintains order and peace. Dreadful like thunder, it prevents any rebellion. But now let me tell you about the sword of the common man." The king sat and listened.

"The sword of the common man is used by those who are tousle-haired with spiky beards, who wear loose caps held on by coarse cords. They have their robes cut short behind. They stare about themselves fiercely and only talk about their swordsmanship. Raised high, this sword cuts through the neck. Swung low, it slices into the liver and lungs. The people who use the sword of the common man are no better than fighting cocks who at any time can have their lives cut off. Now you, Your Majesty, have the position of the Son of Heaven yet you make yourself unworthy by associating with the sword of the common man." On finishing his speech Chuey gave a slight bow of his head.

The king was visibly shaken by Chuey's description of the three swords. He had Chuey brought up to his private rooms where attendants presented trays of food. The agitated king just kept pacing round the room until Chuey said, "Sire, sit down and calm yourself. Whatever there was to say about swords has been said."

The prince said that Chuey's speech had a great effect. He told me that the king had not left the palace since then, though all of the swordsmen were ordered to leave. The prince concluded his story by saying, "Madam, such great service to the state and not one piece of gold would he accept, not one gift, though many were offered." I caught Chuey's eye and directed my eyes down towards his felt fencing boots which were already showing signs of wear. Chuey gave a little smile.

"Yes Madam", the prince paused and shook his head, failing to find words to adequately describe his feelings, "your husband is a truly remarkable man." I stared at Chuey, my mind reeling from the details of the events the prince had just described, and couldn't help but agree.

Chuey treated his trip to the capital as something of a secret. If any of the visitors alluded to it he would quickly move the conversation on to some other topic, but I started to get the feeling that people had come to know something of the story. There was a re-emergence of the 'not-the-prime-minister's-wife' jokes and a renewing of the respect Chuey seemed to command around the town. My suspicions were confirmed when I visited the butcher one day.

I usually only bought meat from the butcher when the hunting and fishing had been unsuccessful, and only if we had any spare money. We could only ever afford a small amount of a cheap cut, but I am sure that the butcher always gave us more than he charged us for. Then one day he cut me a large chunk of the most tender part of the animal. I exclaimed at the mistake but he waved my protests away and put his fingers to his lips to hush my alarm. Under his breath he said, "That's on the house. Make a nice dinner for Chuey. Tell him I said it's for helping out my old mate the king." He gave me a knowing wink and turned to serve the next customer.

It was clear that not everyone was in on the secret. One scholar proved as much. It was the same gloating scholar who had visited us several times before. Each time he had visited he had been keen to 'win', and each time he had taken losing badly. This time he was returning from the state of Chin where he had been sent on a diplomatic mission. He was dressed in clothes even finer than the ones he had worn on his previous visit, intricately embroidered and trimmed with fur. Apparently, he had been given a hundred carriages by the king of Chin as a gift for services rendered. After alighting from the first carriage he waved on the subsequent carriages so the full extent of his success would be apparent.

Chuey greeted him civilly. Once inside, the scholar soon turned the conversation around to praising

Chuey for his stoic endurance of his continuing lack of success. He looked disdainfully round our little home, saying that he was quite sure he would never have the strength to endure such deprivation. His false-modesty was almost sickening as he said that he had no idea why the king of Chin had decided to reward him with so many carriages. He then wafted his hand towards the road to illustrate the point. But outside we could hear shouting. The scholar stood up to see what was happening.

"A hundred you say?" Chuey enquired.

The scholar gave a small smile and a slight nod of his head to acknowledge the compliment, but that had not been Chuey's meaning at all. Chuey and I looked at each other. Chuey added, "Only, it's quite a narrow lane, and there's no real turning circle."

The sounds from outside confirmed Chuey's words as angry shouts and horses' neighing began to herald the farce which was unfolding. The lane is narrow. Turning carriages around at our house always requires careful manoeuvring. For a hundred carriages to come up our tiny track, to turn round and to pass back down again was an impossibility.

We followed our guest as he went out to inspect the carnage. I stood behind Chuey, trying not to grin at the chaos. The scholar was getting flustered. Horses reared as the carriages jammed in the tight space, with the returning carriages being forced off the lane, into the soft wet gravel of the stream bed.

Chuey raised his voice above the mayhem. "A hundred carriages? Well now!"

The scholar turned his head and gave another little grimace, to acknowledge the repeat of the supposed compliment, but Chuey hadn't been intending a compliment this time either.

Chuey continued, "I heard that when the king of Chin falls ill, a doctor who lances an ulcer or squeezes a boil gets one carriage, but the doctor who applies a suppository gets five carriages. So, what have you been up to with the king of Chin to receive a hundred carriages? I assume you must have, at the very least, been tending to his piles! Now be gone, and take your carriages with you!"

With that Chuey opened the door and held it for me to enter, followed me inside then slammed it shut, leaving the scholar to his salvage operation. Inside, we laughed and I remembered how much fun it was being Chuey's wife.

18. ANOTHER FUNERAL

There was one last event from those times that I should mention. Hans, who had gone to court at the personal invitation of the king, killed himself. It happened after he had been imprisoned due to rumours that he was a spy, but it seems these were merely based on him having foreign parents. The king had summoned Hans to court to help with some of the unwelcome advice from his ministers, but the boy with the stutter was no match for the worldly courtiers. Once Hans was in jail, one of the scholars was said to have pressured Hans into taking poison.

The king had been deeply saddened by Hans's death and provided for an elaborate funeral. Mensa and Hussain oversaw the proceedings as by then they were regularly employed as funeral directors. Confucius was no longer around to help his students with the ceremony. A while before that he had undergone a dramatic transformation. The change in my cousin happened after another of his visits to the old man.

Confucius had stayed with Mensa and Kim, as was then usual. I noticed him driving up the lane early one morning. When he arrived he seemed rather depressed. "Greetings Cousin. Alright if I leave the horse here for a while? I'm just going up to see the old man." I asked if anything was wrong. He told me that he had just returned from visiting a foreign state where, once again, he had failed to persuade the ruler to adopt his methods.

I saw Confucius later, walking back down. He morosely informed me that the old man had told him that his whole approach was just bragging. It worried me to see my cousin so dejected, so I suggested that we use his carriage to take a picnic to Chuey and Euan who were at the river. "We can take rods," I offered brightly, hoping that some fishing might help to lighten his mood. Confucius didn't seem too thrilled at the idea but grunted "Alright". I packed some food and we set off.

We found Euan lying on the grassy bank. Chuey was down at the water's edge close by, squatting with his rod. They were pleased to see us, particularly when they noticed the picnic. Chuey brought in his line and we all sat enjoying the food in the warmth of the midday sun.

After we had eaten, Chuey returned to his rod. I thought of joining him, but I wasn't dressed for fishing and I was happy to stay sitting in the sun. The warmth of the day soon made me drowsy and I lay back on the soft grass with my hat over my face. Euan and Confucius were sitting close by, preferring the broken shade of the tree behind.

I heard Confucius sigh, then say to himself in a defeated tone, "I don't know".

Euan doesn't usually say much. He would be the last person I would have expected to react to

Confucius's verbal sigh, so it was a surprise when I heard him say in a low voice, "And what is it that you don't know, Confucius?"

Confucius sighed. "Ah," then he paused as though not knowing where to start. "Well, I've been exiled from Lu, twice. I had a tree toppled on top of me in Sung. All records of me have been wiped out in Wei. I was impoverished in Shang, not to mention besieged in Chen, and then I was besieged again in Tsai! My friends and acquaintances have wandered off and my followers have started to desert me. I don't know. Why does all of this keep happening to me?"

After a pause Euan said quietly, "I have heard that the perfect man is never heard, so why do you feel the need to travel all around, trying to talk to everyone? Confucius, I believe you know little of the Tao."

I was surprised by my cousin's response. "Do you imagine that I do not know that myself?" What followed was even more of a shock. "Could you teach me the Tao?"

Euan chuckled gently. "You certainly have a great love of learning." He paused. "No, I think our paths are too different for that."

"Oh, how can I rid myself of the ills that afflict me and make my mission successful?" lamented Confucius.

It didn't sound like my cousin's forlorn question was aimed at anyone in particular, but Euan seemed happy to continue the conversation. "Your question just shows how far you are from understanding. Confucius, you are like the man who tries to run from his own shadow and from his own footprints. No matter how quickly he runs he cannot get away. Eventually he will drop dead of exhaustion. Whereas if he merely sat in the shade of a large tree the shadow would disappear, and if he remained still his feet would produce no footprints." I heard Euan let out a long, "Ah," and I could imagine him shaking his head.

A moment later Confucius asked plainly, "Then, what am I to do?"

"I don't know Confucius, but when you no longer occupy yourself with yourself, then you will be free from your trials."

"Ha," Confucius laughed in disbelief. "And do you think I could do that?"

After a moment's silence, Euan said "Mm, yes, I do."

No one spoke and the conversation was over.

I heard someone humming. I tipped my hat up and looked up to see who it was. It was Confucius. He seemed a lot brighter. "You know what, I think I will try some fishing after all," he said, suddenly seeming quite merry.

After he had driven us all home I watched Confucius drive away, back down the lane towards the main road, and that was the last time I saw my cousin. I was happy that the fishing trip had lifted his spirits. We heard later that he had gone straight home and had given away all his books. Next, we heard that he had gone to live in a great marsh where he dressed in animal skins and rough cloth, and lived off acorns and chestnuts. Apparently, he became so natural that when he went out amongst the birds and animals they were not afraid of him. When I heard of Confucius's change of style I smiled, remembering the man Chuey had been talking with when I first saw him.

As Hans's funeral began, I was struck by the appearance of Mensa and Hussain. Chuey and I were towards the back, quite a long way from them, but from our position it looked as though the students had learned from their master very well. Seeing them in their robes, with their big sleeves, and walking as though they could hardly lift their feet, they now both looked exactly like Confucius had done at the funeral where I first met Chuey. I heard they had also started a school, or at least they were continuing Confucius's school, which had become quite large, offering lessons on rituals, music, archery, chariot driving, calligraphy and mathematics.

Mo was at the ceremony too. He was accompanied by several of his followers. His strange ideas had started to spread and were growing into something of a new religion. It was nice to think of them all going around preaching universal love, but as Mo had added happiness and crying to his list of bad things it must have been a strange life they led.

Ian had also travelled back for the occasion, meaning that all of the old gang were together for one last time. Ian's pretty wife, and his even prettier young concubine, were with him and, just as the king had predicted, it was obvious that Ian's style of governing his household was not proving too successful. Even at the ceremony the tensions were evident. Despite his troubled home-life, Ian seemed to have achieved his aims of fine clothes, fine food, fine women and a fine house. I don't know whether it made him happy, but much later I heard that his priorities changed and he started taking a more spiritual view of life. That happened after he'd decided, surprisingly, to climb the track beyond our house, to visit the old man.

I scanned the crowd looking for people I knew and spotted Sue, with Dan, sitting on the stage reserved for officials and local dignitaries. They now looked very grand. They had certainly risen a long way from their humble cottage next door to us. We had never moved of course, and we haven't since. I smiled at the comparison as I looked at Chuey, standing there in his worn out, patched up old clothes, and I looked down at my own worn out, patched up old clothes. I can smile at such things now because none of that bothers me much anymore. Yes, I could put more effort into our clothing, but nowadays there always seem to be other, more interesting things to do.

As I looked around at all the other mourners, it seemed as though everyone was living more comfortably than my husband and I. It made me laugh to remember Leah telling me, almost as soon as I'd met Chuey, that the wives and children of those with the Tao can expect to live in comfort. She was wrong! Though, to be fair to Leah, I had the impression that she too was living quite comfortably the last time I saw her.

Leah visited us one year when she brought her grandchildren to see the autumn festival. I was wearing some very fishy fishing clothes when she drove up in a nice carriage. She was smartly dressed. Almost immediately, she mentioned her surprise that we were still living in the same small house. Her eyebrows were still raised when she entered and looked around to see that nothing much had changed inside either. At one time I would have felt Leah's condescending judgement of our home greatly, but not now. Now that the children have homes and families of their own, our house is big enough for the two of us, though when they bring the grandchildren to visit, it turns back into the crowded place of chaos it always used to be. I call it cosy. When I step outside into our valley, I can still feel the wonder I felt the first time I stepped out and saw it all, and I can honestly say that I wouldn't swap our little house for any other house in town, not for the prime minister's house, not even for a palace.

Leah's surprise at our continuing poverty did nothing to spoil the visit. It was great to catch up and it meant I could finally ask her whether her husband could really fly for fifteen days at a time. Her reply was as dry as usual. She said that she didn't know whether he was ever able to fly or not, but she told me that her husband used to sometimes sit in the middle of the floor for up to fifteen days at a time.

It had been quite annoying for the family apparently, who were forced to walk round him. She added that if he had managed to fly, he hadn't flown very far. As to whether he was the 'Transcendent Master of the Void', all she could say was that he was certainly the 'Master of aVoiding work'. Leah was acting the same role she had always done earlier in her life, but there was a fondness in her words now and I sensed that her own resentment at our husbands' strange priorities had also softened with time.

I got a clue about Leah's fine carriage and clothes when she mentioned that the 'flying' had been good for business. She said that the visitors all came claiming to be on a quest for wisdom, but most of them actually just wanted to learn how to fly. I had once wondered whether Leah's husband had more of the Tao than Chuey but, looking at her fine clothes, I guessed that their comfortable lifestyle had more to do with Leah having the Tao of business in a way that I never possessed.

We still get plenty of visitors of our own of course, but none of Chuey's visitors could ever be considered in any way 'good for business'. We recently had Uncle Toothless knock on the door. He isn't a relation, that's just his name. I had often seen him shuffling around town with his walking stick, but we had never met. When he arrived, he explained that he thought that, seeing as he was getting so old, he ought to hear about the Tao before he died. Chuey seemed surprised at his reasoning but sat him down by the fire anyway.

I heard Chuey start telling Uncle Toothless about the Tao and gaining control of the body and its organs, and of bringing the mind to one-pointedness, and how the harmony of Heaven will then come down to dwell in you. After a while Chuey stopped talking. I looked over and saw why the lesson had ended. Uncle Toothless had fallen asleep. Soon a rasping noise started coming from his open mouth. Chuey was delighted. "Who can compare with this toothless old man?" he whispered. "This man has true wisdom!" Chuey crept away, leaving Uncle Toothless to enjoy his nap by the fire.

Back in the days when the pressing needs of our growing family seemed like our only priority, that would have made me angry. Nowadays, even the dourest of discussions on Tao don't distress me. If I do start to feel any of my old annoyance, like if someone starts talking about nothingness or anyone starts telling anyone about starlight asking questions, I usually go off fishing, or I go and sweep out the ancestor shrine. I see Chuey's Tao discussions for what they are. Tao is just a word he uses. Chuey summed it up just last night actually, when an earnest young man knocked on our door asking for directions to the old man's house. He had brought his wife along, would you believe, and she was clearly pregnant. As it was already late in the day Chuey suggested they leave the ascent until morning. So, yet again, we shared our home and our dinner.

We all settled down around the fire and the conversation started to flow, but it was soon dominated by the young man's interest in the Tao. As he pressed Chuey with his insistent questions, I watched the young wife. She was a delicate, mouse of a girl. I saw her glancing around the house nervously. It took me back to so long ago, when I had first sat at that fireside discovering the man I had married and coping with my own worries and insecurities. It was as though I was watching myself all those years before. I sighed for my young guest, not sure how I could help her but very much wanting to.

The two men continued to discuss the Tao, but I could tell that Chuey was getting tired of his conversation with such an intense interrogator. With some force he said, "Look, the word Tao is just a word. It is a limited term. It cannot describe the unlimited. The idea of the Tao simply takes us to the edge. The edge of what? Neither words nor silence are able to describe this. That is why no words, no silence, is the highest form of debate." The young man was silent. I found myself nodding. I held a moment of eye-contact with the wife and smiled. She smiled back.

After all these years with Chuey, that is how I see it. Nowadays I don't mind people taking his time with their discussions about the Tao. If people want to talk about the Tao, Chuey talks about the Tao. Like the man who the old man described, Chuey is the same whether he's talking about the Tao or not. He's the same in the morning, in the afternoon and evening, and he's the same when he sleeps at night. Tao is just a word he uses sometimes, a word representing an idea, an idea of something beyond words. It takes us to the edge of what can be talked about, so we can help each other to be with that which is beyond, to help us appreciate this magical world that we all live in. Once we see things like that, the word can be forgotten. Beyond the word, you can wander where you will, without needing a path. There, you might even perceive Chuey's teacher. That is where Chuey lives. He doesn't just fly for fifteen days, he is always flying. He never lands. He doesn't even know whether he is really Chuey or a dreaming butterfly. I don't suppose he even wants to know. He can't explain how he lives and how he sees it all, all he can do is to use a little word to help give people an idea. Yes, his ideas are too big to be useful, but like he said, use them to enjoy floating down the current. I have seen him do it. I'm better at doing it myself now. Now, I can even begin to see that perhaps he does know the happiness of fishes, just by being there.

I used to doubt that Chuey really loved me. As his wife, that worried me. Now I see that it's just that I have to share his love with the whole of everything. That's fine. And as I've come to love the whole of everything more myself, it's only fair. It takes nothing away. It only adds. Yes, I'm very happy to be Chuey's wife, and I know that Chuey is very happy to be my husband.

EPILOGUE

Mei looked at her host and nodded to acknowledge the learning she had received. The woman smiled back at her guest and dipped her head almost imperceptibly to acknowledge the acknowledgement.

A moment later, the door opened and the woman's husband entered. He quickly shut the door to keep out the cold wind. With a shiver, he greeted the women and went over to them to warm himself at the fire.

The older woman picked up the empty jug. Without a shred of remorse she laughed, "I'm sorry Chuey, I hope you weren't wanting any wine. I'm afraid we've drunk it all!"

END PIECE

When Chuey's wife died, Hue went to the house to console him. To his surprise he found Chuey sitting on the ground with an inverted bowl between his knees. He was bashing it and singing a song.

"This is not right Chuey! After all," said Hue, "she lived with you, brought up your children and grew old with you. Not to mourn for her is bad enough, but to let your friends find you drumming and singing – that is too much!"

"You misjudge me," said Chuey. "When she died, I was in despair, as any man well might be. But I thought back to her birth and to the very roots of her being before she was born. Indeed, not just before she was born but before her body was created, before the very origin of her life's breath. I told myself that in death no strange new fate befalls us. In the beginning we lack not life only, but form. Not form only, but spirit. We are blended in the one great featureless indistinguishable mass. Then a time came when the mass evolved spirit, spirit evolved form, form evolved life. Now there is yet another transformation and she is departed. Man's being has its seasons, its sequence of spring and autumn, summer and winter. If someone is tired and has gone to lie down, we do not pursue them with shouting and bawling. She whom I have lost has lain down to sleep for a while in the Great Inner Room. Why should I break in upon her rest with noisy lamentation as though I knew nothing of nature's Sovereign Law?"

THE END

AUTHOR'S AFTERWORD

The Mystic's Wife has been woven from characters and anecdotes taken mainly from an ancient Chinese book called the *Chuang Tzu,* (or Zhuangzi in the pinyin system). The *Chuang Tzu* comes from the period of 'The Hundred Schools of Thought' and is thought to date from the last half of the fourth century BCE. In particular, the End Piece of *The Mystic's Wife* comes directly from the *Chuang Tzu* – only the two names have been changed.

Chuang Tzu contains tales and essays collected around the historical figure of that name, also known as Chuang Chou, Kwang-Tze, or Zhuangzi. Chuey is the character playing his part in *The Mystic's Wife.* Chuang Tzu lived with his wife and family in one of the warring states that would eventually form China. (The description of Chuang Tzu 'mourning' for his wife can be found in Chapter 18 of the *Chuang Tzu.* It is the only mention of Chuang Tzu's wife.) His friend and debating foil was Hui Tzu. Hue has been playing his part.

I wanted to write this novel to share some of the *Chuang Tzu's* fun and philosophy that I feel I have benefitted from. I thought it would be nice to hear Chuang Tzu's wife telling her side of the story. It sounds as though she had quite a lot to contend with and I'm guessing that she might have had a slightly different perspective on some of the events described in the *Chuang Tzu* compared to that of her husband. As we hear her character saying here, "No one is just someone's wife." She was a person and she would have needed to find her own way to get along with her husband's strange and sometimes challenging worldview. At the back of my mind, or perhaps at the top, is the hope that hearing Chuey's wife tell her story might help someone else to cope with living with that mystic who we all have to live with: the one that each one of us has inside. On that quest, other people's words might sometimes help, and sometimes they might not, but either way other people's words can't be the whole story. In the end, each one of us has to find our own way. That journey is what *The Mystic's Wife* is really about.

If you have enjoyed *The Mystic's Wife*, or if you've found it somehow useful, you might want to delve into the sources a little. I should warn you that the *Chuang Tzu* is a varied collection. Some of its pieces are considerably less interesting than others – reading it 'cover to cover' would be an undertaking for an enthusiast. I found Thomas Merton's poetic rendering of selected parts of the *Chuang Tzu*, called *The Way of Chuang Tzu*, to be a beautiful introduction.

As far as we know, Chuang Tzu's wife was a real person. Many of the other characters in *The Mystic's Wife* are also loosely based on historical figures from

Ancient China. As fabricator of this work of fiction, I feel I should offer apologies to these real people and clearly state that the characters presented here are not intended to be true representations of those individuals. Rather, I am following the author(s) of the *Chuang Tzu*, both in the content and the 'looseness' of the content. For example, the character of Confucius is based firmly on the character of that name who appears in the *Chuang Tzu* and has very little to do with the historical details of man who inspired Confucianism. I have read that Confucius appears in the *Chuang Tzu* more often than Chuang Tzu himself. I haven't counted the number of times myself, but he certainly crops up a lot. He is sometimes presented almost as the 'butt of the joke', but the author(s) of the *Chuang Tzu* seem to have had a genuine fondness and respect for him. I have tried to reflect this in *The Mystic's Wife*, using anecdotes and descriptions from the *Chuang Tzu* along with additional details from Confucian works such as *The Analects of Confucius*. There is no disrespect intended towards the real Confucius or to any of the other individuals involved. My aim has been merely to pass on a feel for the strange and wonderful world that I have enjoyed discovering through my own reading of the *Chuang Tzu* and related texts.

So, apologies to:

- Chuang Tzu's wife, and to her husband, Chuang Tzu;

- Hui Tzu;

- Lieh Tzu and his wife, (who probably wasn't called Leah);

- Kung Tzu (called Confucius in the West);

- Kung Tzu's favourite follower, Yen Yuan;

- Mo Tzu, Meng Tzu (called Mencius in the West), Han Fei Tzu, Hsun Tzu and Yang Tzu;

- Lao Tzu, the 'Old Master' – Most of the old man's sayings and the quotes inserted between some of the chapters come from James Legge's classic translation of the *Tao Te Ching*, another of the fundamental texts of Taoism;

- Jie Yu (the madman of Chu) and Kung Yueh Hsiu (who speared turtles in winter);

- Sun Tzu;

- And to any other real people bearing any resemblance to any of the characters in this book.

And I'd like to offer my sincere thanks to:

- The author(s) of the *Chuang Tzu* and to authors of all the other books from Ancient China that have influenced *The Mystic's Wife*;

* All the commentators and translators down through the centuries, who have passed on their understanding of these texts;

* Also to all the transcribers and people who preserved the physical copies of these books, enabling us modern people to enjoy these ideas and this view of a time and place that is a world away from our own, yet which seems to me to be in many ways rather similar.

Tima Lee

8th August 2023

A MESSAGE FROM EARTHENWARE BOOKS

The Mystic's Wife is unlikely to receive much mainstream promotion. If you know of anyone who might enjoy reading it, or anyone who might somehow benefit from reading it, please let them know about this book.
Thanks

EARTHENWARE BOOKS

Printed in Great Britain
by Amazon